Also by Levitt & Kent

A Labour pn/Sn
Though by Opposition
Labor by Desire
Normal

Also by Lavinia Kent

A Talent for Sin
Bound by Temptation
Taken by Desire
Norma

The Real Duchesses of London

KATHRYN, THE KITTEN

LAVINIA KENT

This book is a work of fiction. The characters, incidents, and dialogue are drawn from the author's imagination and are not to be construed as real. Any resemblance to actual events or persons, living or dead, is entirely coincidental.

KATHRYN, THE KITTEN. Copyright © 2011 by Lavinia Kent. All rights reserved under International and Pan-American Copyright Conventions. By payment of the required fees, you have been granted the non-exclusive, non-transferable right to access and read the text of this e-book on-screen. No part of this text may be reproduced, transmitted, down-loaded, decompiled, reverse engineered, or stored in or introduced into any information storage and retrieval system, in any form or by any means, whether electronic or mechanical, now known or hereinafter invented, without the express written permission of HarperCollins e-books.

EPub Edition July 2011 ISBN: 9780062107923

Print Edition ISBN: 9780062115447

10 9 8 7 6 5 4 3

The Real Duchesses of London*

Kathryn, The Duchess of Harrington
"I am the perfect duchess. I am beautiful, rich, well read, well spoken, and have a civilized relationship with the duke. What more could a woman want?"

Elizabeth, The Countess of Westhampton
"I may not be a duchess, but I am more of a lady than any of them. You'll never see me in the scandal sheets. Mind you, I am not saying I haven't ever been scandalous—just that you'll never know."

Georgianna, Lady Richard Tennant
"My son will be a duke. It doesn't matter if I get to be a duchess as long as I know my son will inherit from his uncle, will hold the title. My husband may have broken many of his promises to me, but that one is absolute."

Linnette, The Dowager Duchess of Doveshire
"I have no intention of giving up what is mine. I've run the house and the estates for years. Why would I ever give them up now? I don't care who the new duke is."

Annabelle, The Marchioness of Tattingstong

"They say that, because I am American, I have no taste, no grace, no style, no refinement. I have every intention of showing them just how wrong they are—and when the time comes, I will be the perfect duchess."

*All quotes as relayed to Miss Jane White, more or perhaps less accurately, by Miss Mary White, lady's maid for the Duchess of Harrington

The Maids

"Oh lordy, do you think they really look like that? Like a cross between angels and fence posts?" Abby asked, reaching out to trace the print in the apothecary's window with a finger, her cheeks pink with interest. The street was not yet crowded at this early morning hour and it was possible to stop and stare at the crowded display on the glass.

"You're smudging the window, but you do have the most vivid imagination. I would never have thought angels and fence posts could have any relationship, but you are correct. That is exactly what they look like in the print," Jane White answered as she inched up on her toes to stare more closely at the black-and-white print hanging among the cartoons in the window, turning her back on her fellow maid. She stared at the tall, dark-haired woman in the center of the print. Her hair was caught up in a mass of curls and pearls shone at her throat. "I do know that is what the Duchess of Harrington looks like. My sister has recently found employment in her house and I saw the duchess last week when I was visiting. I was making my way to the back when her carriage pulled up in front. Of course, I had to stay and watch her come out. You've never seen such a fine lady—and yes, her back was just like a fence post. I don't know how anyone can stand so straight."

"Maybe she wears an old corset. My mother always spoke of ones that could stand up by themselves." Abby peered up at the drawing, wrinkling her brow. "I'd forgotten that was where Mary had found a position. She always did do well for herself, that sister of yours—and she does have a knack with hair. I bet she's even a lady's maid—not stuck down in the kitchens like me or even a parlor maid like you. But why does the title say 'The Real Duchesses of London'? If they're duchesses, they're duchesses, why say real? I will never understand the upstairs lot."

Jane came down off her toes and turned to Abby. "I think it says real duchesses because they're not all actually duchesses—not that that makes any sense either. I know that one, the one in the hat with all the feathers, is the Marchioness of Tattingstong. She was in the cartoons when she married the marquess. Don't you remember the ones where she was holding out a fishing rod with a bucket of money on the end? She's American and it was most shocking when Lord Tattingstong came back from his travels with her. Of course, he was only a second son when he became engaged. Can you imagine how his father, the duke, felt?"

"That's her? You're right, it is. I should have recognized her profile."

"Profile? I don't see why— Oh, you mean her whole profile. She does have remarkable bosoms. Normally they show them sticking out even further with an American flag between them."

"There's no flag this time. Do you think she really wears one? I always thought it was just a bit of humor."

"I am sure that she doesn't wear one all the time—if at all. I think it's not in this one because it's not really a cartoon. I imagine they really look like this."

Jane stepped back and considered the print. The five women were so similar and so distinctly different at the same time. They all looked as if they knew some secret that every other woman in the world wanted to know. It was hard to say what gave that impression. Their gowns were certainly fine and Jane could not have paid for one of those bonnets with a year's salary. The jewels that adorned their ears, and wrists, and necks were probably even more dear, but the print failed to capture the full sparkle and glory of the gems.

But it was none of this that gave the duchesses their secret look. It was something in their eyes or perhaps their mouths. Was it that slight up-tilt of lip? The way they held their chins, angled the barest fraction higher than the rest of humanity? Perhaps it was their shoulders? Jane had seen plenty of aristocrats, but none who held themselves with such perfection of bearing. These women were queens and they knew it.

For a moment she wondered if it could be the artist's imagination, if he'd added a little something extra to them as he'd drawn them. No, when she'd seen Her Grace of Harrington, she'd had that exact look as she'd glided into the house.

Jane leaned even closer, trying to understand the secret.

"Be careful or you'll go right through the window," Abby cautioned.

Jane stepped back. "I am trying to understand what makes them so special."

"It's all the gowns and money. That's an easy one to answer. Give me a gown like that and I would fit right in." Abby thrust her nose in the air, pulled her shoulders back, and spun in a circle.

Jane suppressed her giggle. Abby was a dear friend and it would not do to hurt her feelings, but the image of her as a duchess, with her frizz of brown hair and button nose, was impossible. And that was not even considering the angle of her front teeth.

No, there was something else about the women. She glanced at her own reflection in the glass, lifted her chest, turned her body to the side, tilted her chin just slightly, imitating the pose of the Duchess of Harrington. She tried to imagine herself dressed in emerald silk—somehow she just knew the duchess's dress was green—diamonds flashing at her ears and neck, a handsome duke waiting to escort her.

This time she could not hold back her laugh. The thought of her barely five-foot frame draped in silk was too much to imagine—and that was without even imagining the six-foot-plus Duke of Harrington coming her way.

Abby looked up at the print again. "You've pointed out the Duchess of Harrington and the Marchioness of Tattingstong, but who are the others?"

"I am not really sure. That one looks a little like the Dowager Duchess of Doveshire. I've never seen her but there were drawings when her husband died and she kept running the duchy and the new duke stayed in India—and then he died too. I wonder if there's a new duke?"

Abby gave a cheeky smile. "It seems like there should be a limerick about that. You must be able to do something with two dead dukes."

"Stop that, Abby, if you're not careful, you'll slip and say something in the kitchen and you know how Cook will react. She hates it when we joke about our betters. And we'd best be getting on our way. We were sent out to search for more flowers not to..."

Abby reached out and traced the Marchioness's feathers with her fingers one last time. "I normally hate that term—*betters*. But, there is something about them. What was the word you used—*special?* There is something special about them. You are right, though, we'd best be on our way."

Jane turned her head to look at the print one last time. It stood out clearly among the many others. Then, turning away from the glass, she smiled at Abby. "I suppose I'll never know what makes them different, special—but you know, they don't actually look altogether happy."

Chapter One

Kathryn Cottsworth, Duchess of Harrington, looked down at the lush gown spread across her bed and pursed her lips. The heavy green silk with the rich cream lace was one of her favorites. She'd worn it to three balls and a dinner and didn't care. It suited her perfectly and what was the point in being a duchess if one couldn't wear what one wished—even if she had worn it before?

She glanced at the copy of the print that on the table. This, though, this was too much. The print was up in shop windows! She'd never had such an experience before and didn't relish it now. It wasn't a horrible cartoon, but her mother had always been clear that a lady avoided publicity. She should only be in the papers for her birth, her wedding announcement, and her death—anything more was vulgar.

A print in the apothecary's window wasn't the papers, but she had a feeling her mother would have thought it was worse. Only women with scandalous reputations appeared in cartoons. This, however, wasn't a cartoon, she told herself again. It looked almost like the drawings she'd done as schoolgirl of her mother and her aunts. Although this artist was clearly more talented, she could almost hear conversation as she glanced at the paper. And she'd never even been together with these women in one group.

She ran a finger over the silk dress again. It was cool and sleek beneath her touch, so comfortable no matter how hot the summer grew.

She wished she knew some appropriate curses. "Bloody hell" might be suitable, but she could never let such words pass her lips—at least not when she was observed. Her gaze shifted to her new lady's maid, Mary. "I suppose you can take the dress and dispose of it in whatever manner you see fit." She caught Mary's eyes and stared hard. "As long as I never see or hear of it again."

"As you wish, your grace." Mary dropped her gaze and nodded. It was clear she'd also heard the unfortunate story of the Countess of Nevilles, who'd arrived at the opera to discover her husband's mistress attired in one of her old gowns. The story had passed from lip to lip for weeks.

Not that Robert would ever do such a thing to her. He was much too civil—and discreet. She wasn't even sure that he had a mistress. She imagined that he must, a man like Robert had women chasing him wherever he went. He'd had a mistress before they were wed, even if she didn't know whom. Robert might be civil, but he was still a man and men had needs—and he certainly wasn't meeting them with her—at least not very often.

A soft sigh escaped her lips, as she again brushed a finger across the silk.

Early in their marriage she'd welcomed him to her bed twice a week, or even more often, unless she was indisposed, but since the tragedy, she was lucky if she even saw him in private that often. Her hand dropped to her belly and she forced it away. She would not think of that—of what could never be.

She turned back to Mary and watched as she folded the silk with care. It would fetch a pretty penny at some market stall or wherever it was maids took such things.

Walking toward the window, she stared out at the scene below, perfect gardens, perfect street, perfect square across the way. Her gaze dropped lower to the pale stones that made up the house's exterior wall. Perfect house, perfect vines, perfect window. She spun back to the room, to all the elegant furniture and fine appointments. She'd had it redone in the softest blue this past year and it too was perfect. Not a wrinkle marked the coverlet, not a speck of dust on any surface, every pane of glass, crystal goblet, or mirror sparkling. The single bud that Robert had brought to her each morning a solitary bright spot of crimson.

She walked across the room and stared into the mirror. Rich, dark hair piled high with only two gold and pearl combs visible. Neck held so straight and narrow she sometimes wondered if it still remembered how to bend. Breasts softly curved, but well covered given the time of day. A simple cameo and one strand of pearls adorned her high-waisted wool dress, the deep blue of the fabric a perfect match for the room. Her gaze swept down the dress, stopping at her waist, just as narrow as it had been before—no, she had already decided not to think of that. Her skirts, like the coverlet, were still without wrinkle or crease despite the hours she'd been wearing them, her slippers invisible beneath her hems.

Yes, she too was perfect.

She bent forward, staring at rosebud lips and cheeks, pale skin beneath eyes the color of darkest chocolate. She'd been the reigning beauty the year she'd come out, despite being almost on the shelf, and the year after that as well. No one had come close to touching her.

The daughter of a duke, the granddaughter of two dukes, she'd snared another for a husband.

Perfect, simply perfect.

Except she wasn't.

With great deliberation she placed both hands on her flat stomach.

She didn't want to think of it, but she had to—there was no other way to get what she wanted, what she needed.

The duke needed an heir and she had not managed to deliver, her one great task in life and she had failed.

She closed her eyes at the memory of the pain, of the blood, of the pale, unbreathing flesh, of Robert turning away without a word.

He'd never said anything about it. Every trace of the expected child had vanished before she was out of bed and not a word had been said by anyone—except the physician who told her brusquely that after a few months she could try again.

That had been well over a year ago.

She opened her eyes and batted her lashes quickly against the tears that threatened, that had threatened for well over a year now.

A perfect duchess did not cry.

And they had tried again, she and Robert, not as often as those first months, but with some, if ever decreasing, regularity. And nothing had happened. Nothing.

Nothing. A word that seemed to fill her life.

It had happened so fast that first time. Could something inside her be damaged?

She pressed her hands harder against her empty belly.

It had been almost three months since her husband had come to her at night.

Pulling in a deep breath, she met her own gaze.

It could not continue. Robert was the duke. She was the duchess.

The task must be completed.

"I hear that old Freddy is expecting his tenth. I can't even imagine how his wife makes it past his belly."

The *sotto voce* whisper filled the dark comfort of the club and Robert froze, refusing to betray by even a single blink that he found the words disturbing. He turned his full attention to his newspaper, ignoring the even more ribald comments that followed. He did not want to think about other men and their children. In fact, he didn't want to think at all.

He forced his eyes to focus on the paper in front of him, sinking behind the wings of his chair, seeking something to draw his attention. France was still moaning about the death of Napoleon. Oh, they phrased it differently, but he knew a moan when he heard one. Mexico was still attempting to fight Spain for independence. He knew that already and was frankly tired of reading about war. There was a new exhibition at the Royal Academe. He read a brief description of the show. It didn't sound interesting to him. He thought of himself as a modern man in most ways, but he liked the art his father and his grandfather had liked—good solid portraits, people and horses. His wife would probably like these, though. Kathryn had always enjoyed the edge of something new. He should mention the exhibition to her.

Maybe it was time to get her portrait painted. She'd been his duchess for over two years now. He'd always planned to have her painted with their first child in her . . .

Damnation, he was thinking about children again—about children and Kathryn. He'd spent the last year working hard to think about neither—although the harder he worked at not thinking about his duchess, the more he seemed to dream about her, about her velvet skin, her sweet smile, the way she curled up in her bed like a kitten, a soft, purring kitten and he dreamed of the gentle hands he'd always longed to have . . .

He folded the paper and placed it neatly on the table beside him. Almost before he'd finished the movement, Smits, the club's steward, appeared, decanter in hand. "Would you care for some brandy, your grace?"

Robert hesitated. He never drank this early in the day. He'd seen with his father just how easy it was for a single glass to turn into ten far too many times. "Yes, I'll have one."

The amber liquid flowed into the glass, the reassuring sweet odor burning his nostrils. He lifted the glass and stared at it, waving Smits away. It would be easy to lose himself in it. There were, however, responsibilities awaiting him that could not be put off for another day. If he didn't decide between a canal and a newfangled railroad soon he'd lose his chance to persuade the Dowager Duchess of Doveshire to join him in creating a new way of getting all their goods to market. He had sway with Linnette, she was easy to persuade—if the new duke were found, first things would be considerably more complicated and delayed.

He took another steep swallow.

"I am surprised to see you here, Harrington. I didn't think you the type to haunt this place at such an early hour." Thomas Nettingsly, the Marquess of Tattingstong, pulled a high wing chair to the other side of the table. He leaned forward, elbows on the table, just as he had years ago when they'd been at school.

"My mother and grandmother have both arrived in Town today." Which was cause for another swallow.

"They are staying with you?" Tattingstong asked.

"Where else?" A large gulp.

"I do understand your flight then. I always make myself scarce when my own mother comes to call and she is nothing compared to . . ." Tattingstong let his words trail off.

"Don't be afraid of insulting either of the dowager duchesses. I know your words are true and my mother would probably take pride in them. And who knows what my grandmother thinks? I don't believe she considers me worthy of her thoughts."

Tattingstong did not reply, but nodded his acceptance of Robert's statement. The dowager duchess, Robert's mother, had never been an easy woman and since his father's death had been even less so. She had not relished giving up her power as duchess and to this day continued to fight for it.

"Are you not expected to be home to greet them?"

Robert glanced at the clock on the high mantel and considered. His presence was not required. The ladies would arrive in a flurry of trunks and spend the rest of the day making themselves situated. His only purpose would be to listen to their complaints—that seemed to always be his purpose where his mother was concerned.

But if he weren't there, then his mother would turn her complaints on Kathryn. Kathryn would never say a word to him about it and would manage each complaint in her usual practical manner. Everything would be perfect when he got home.

With Kathryn things were always perfect—at least everything but him.

He looked across the table at Tattingstong who was beckoning Smits over. The man looked much too satisfied, satisfied in a way he couldn't remember feeling in over a year. "You are correct. I had best be on my way. I am sure my mother will be anxious to greet me." She wouldn't be, but it might spare Kathryn some bother.

Tattingstong turned back to him and lost the look of satisfaction. He hesitated and then stated, "Actually, I'd come to ask you a favor."

That could be interesting. "Yes?"

"You know, of course, that my wife, that Lady Tattingstong, is new to town."

"Yes." New to the whole country, more like it. What had Tattingstong been thinking of, marrying an American—even if her family did own enough lumber to rebuild the fleet?

"Well—umm... Annabelle, that is, Lady Tattingstong, is having a difficult time—a less than easy time—finding her way through the society we move in. I wondered if perhaps you could ask the duchess to invite her to tea with a few friends and help to smooth the way a bit. I hadn't thought of asking, but then I saw a print of them together and..."

"Yes, I have seen the print. Brooks showed me this morning. I am not certain I really understand what its purpose is." He paused, "And I am just not sure about asking my wife to extend an invitation. I've never tried to suggest to my duchess who her friends should be. I've always found that women understand some code we will never comprehend. And besides Lady Tattingstong is—is . . ."

". . . is American? Believe me, I know. That's all I ever hear from my mother. Why does nobody ever mention that her grandfather was the second son of a duke who left to make his fortune—and succeeded? Her grandmother's bloodlines were impeccable as well. Why does nobody ever mention that?"

"Well . . ." Robert hesitated, unsure what else to say to his friend. He didn't personally mind Americans, but he wasn't sure that he would have married one—not that he'd ever wanted to marry anyone besides Kathryn.

If Kathryn were here, she'd know what to say. Kathryn always had the correct reply. She was also always kind and gracious. Still, he hesitated.

"Please, Robert. I need you to do this for me."

Robert raised his head and stared hard at Tattingstong. He hadn't been called by his first name since they were schoolboys—small boys who'd decided to all be the same by putting aside their honor titles when alone. "It means that much to you?"

"It means the world to me."

"All I can do is ask Kathryn. I will not pressure her."

"That is all I ask."

Chapter Two

"Is it really that bad?" Robert asked as he observed his wife at the top of the stairs. There was nothing to obviously display her unhappiness, but he could see the tension in her shoulders and in that little line that settled between her eyes.

Kathryn turned to him, one hand grasping the railing. Her face relaxed, but he could see that it cost effort. She took a step down toward him. "No, nothing is wrong. Whatever could be wrong?"

He glanced towards the parlor. He'd seen the swish of his mother's skirts as he entered. He took a couple of steps closer to Kathryn and spoke softly. "I know that having guests can be tiring."

She moved further down the stairs, her skirts winding about her long legs. Her gown was a soft lilac. It was higher cut than he liked, her breasts hidden almost completely from his view. He longed for the days when a lucky man could catch the pink edge of a nipple—not that Kathryn had ever been so daring. But mystery had its own allure. And she'd certainly been worth waiting for on those rare occasions that she'd granted him a glance. He shifted, uncomfortable, as his mind filled with the image of her delicate peach-tipped breast—just the perfect size for his hands and . . . No, that was fantasy. She'd never indicated any desire for . . .

He forced his wandering mind back to the present. She must not have changed for dinner yet. That explained the high-necked dress. God, she was beautiful. Every time he saw her his breath caught anew. He'd wanted her since the first moment he'd seen her across a ballroom, and his desire was no less now. If only—

"It would not be so tiring if you joined us for dinner. You could provide quite the distraction." Kathryn said, her voice low, as if sharing a secret. He'd always loved that about her, her ability to create a bubble fitting just the two of them. "I know your mother would love to see more of you. She is not too weary from her travels."

"You mean she would love to complain to me—and about me." Reality settled more firmly about him. He glanced toward the parlor. The private bubble popped—he would not put it past his mother to be listening at the door. "Every time I approach her it just seems to rile her up. It only took five minutes this afternoon for her to turn redder than an apple. I fear that I only make it more difficult for all when I am here."

"I can assure you, your grace, that you do not." She stepped closer, her sweet floral scent wafting about.

Two years and he still wasn't sure what she smelled of. Rose? No. Lavender? No. Honeysuckle? "Have I displeased you too, Kathryn? You normally call me Robert."

There were only a few feet between them now. Kathryn's eyes seemed to measure the space. Before they were married, she would have rushed across it and thrown herself into his arms. He would have clasped her tight, feeling every inch of her delectable body pressed against his, the scent of a sunshine-filled meadow rising from her hair. He might even have dared to nibble her ear, her perfect little shell-like ear. He could almost feel its curves against his lips, imagine . . .

But that had been before they were married, and certainly before . . .

Kathryn placed a hand upon his sleeve, her touch lighter than a butterfly's kiss. "No, you have not displeased me. I believe I have merely been speaking with your mother and grandmother for too long, the endless 'your graces' are filling my head."

"Then you are displeased. Not that I blame you. I truly am busy this evening, but I admit to not be sorry for it." He took a half step closer, waiting to see if she would retreat.

She stayed still, her feet planted. "Then you really must be away for dinner?"

"Yes, I am afraid so."

She took a half step back and then moved forward again. "And after?"

Did she know what she promised when she puckered her lips like that? No, he knew that she did not. Why had he fallen in love with an innocent woman? A woman he seemed bound to hurt? He looked away: sometimes not looking at her was the only way to keep his control. Perhaps he should seek out a mistress. He'd probably scare Kathryn half to death if he acted on even a few of the thoughts that filled his mind when she was so close. "I planned to stay at the club for a few hands of cards. Lord Richard Tennant will be stopping by."

"Oh." She dropped her gaze from his, her shoulders

slumped slightly. Then her head rose again. "Mr. Johns informed me that we've received some new port. Perhaps you would like to come by my room for a glass when you return?" She inched even closer, her face shining with faith and hope—but not desire, never desire.

Why did she not desire him? Other women wanted him. Oh, Kathryn was not unwilling, but she made it clear that it was her duty, both to bed him and to bear him a son.

God, another pregnancy! How could he do that to her? How could he do that to himself? He knew that both she—and his mother—were right that he did need a son, but—but that could wait. They had plenty of time. When she stopped looking at him with such shadows of pain, then they could think about it. "I will be back late. It would be a shame for you to wait up. Why don't you have Mr. Johns leave me a glass by my bed."

"I will do that." Her voice was very small and he could see her wilt like an unwatered flower in the summer sun. And then she stroked his arm, looking up high into his eyes. "Take care, Robert. I will entertain your mother and perhaps your grandmother."

"I know you will." He wanted to say something, do something. "I spoke with the Tattingstong today. He was wondering if you might have his wife to tea. She seems in need of company."

She looked up, her eyes still shadowed. "Is it about that horrid print in all the store windows? I hope you were not too upset by it."

"No, not at all. How could I be upset by anything that makes you look so beautiful? I am only bothered if it worried you."

Her lips turned up in an attempt at a smile. "No, I will be fine. I've just never been featured in anything like it before."

"I know." He wanted to reach out and give her the hug she so badly needed but did not wish to risk her stiffening beneath his touch. Kathryn had rarely been one for physical expression.

She squeezed his arm lightly, as if trying to reassure him. "I will have tea with those you wish and do my best to befriend them."

He jerked back, her kindness hitting him low. She was trying to help and all he could think about was how easy it would be to pull her into his arms, to crush her to him. He really was an animal where his wife was concerned.

She froze as he pulled away, her eyes clouding over—was that pain he saw? Then she collected herself, and when she spoke, her voice was firmer than he'd heard in months. "Yes, Robert, I will entertain your mother and grandmother. I will be a friend with those you wish." Then she softened as if holding strong were too exhausting, and when she spoke, it was with great care, quiet and precise. "But please remember, I am not endless. I always thought I was but I begin to feel my edges."

Her gazed dropped.

Why did he keep hurting her? Sometimes it seemed that she saw that inner beast he worked so hard to keep hidden. It was always the last thing he intended and yet it seemed hopeless. From the moment of their wedding, or at least their wedding night, he seemed bound to cause her injury. He'd always avoided innocents before her. It was the gentlemanly thing to do, but it had left him with no knowledge of how to help the scared young maiden he'd found in his bed that night.

Her fingers were cold where they still held him. They'd

been like icicles on his wedding night. Her whole body had been frozen, stiff unmoving ice. He'd worked hard not to hurt her and by and large thought he had succeeded, but the ice had remained.

He did not think she was frigid—merely unknowing. But then she'd gotten with child so quickly and been so ill. He'd come to bed so many times to hold her, but she always seemed to expect the act when he slipped between her sheets. She'd lie there pale and ill and it was all he could do to complete what was expected of him.

"I know you are not endless, Kathryn." The words felt torn from his chest. "I see you clearly defined. I am sorry that I seem so prone to pushing at your boundaries. I know I have a habit of taking all that is given. I will try to do better. And know I must leave. Lord Richard will be waiting." He pulled from her fingers, and grabbing his hat, prepared to leave.

"Robert, I didn't mean . . ."

And he couldn't let it stop at that. He turned back to her. "Kathryn, let us just get through these days while my mother is here. I do not want to make decisions while she is about. Perhaps, when she is gone, we can head to the country for a few days. A few days with only the two of us. How does that sound?"

Her soft, worried smile was all the answer he needed.

"Oh, I am so pleased that you could come on such short notice." Kathryn rose to greet her guest. Linnette, the Dowager Duchess of Doveshire, had been her friend since before she could remember. They had first met walking, or in her case perhaps toddling, in the park with their nurses and had been inseparable ever since. What she needed to discuss now, however, was far from their childhood ramblings.

She'd felt so barren, in so many ways, after Robert had left last night. Her whole life had stretched before her filled with nothing but one pleasant, insincere smile after another. She'd tried with Robert and failed. She'd invited him to her bed and he'd refused. What was left but unfelt smiles?

And then she'd thought of Linnette—Linnette with her lush body, and husky laugh, with her deep copper curls always dancing in fun. Linnette was a lady, nobody doubted that, but she still carried with her that mysterious quality of—of— there must be a word for that look that told a man she wanted him and wanted him now. Linnette shone with desire, and desirability, and yet always stayed well within the boundaries of decorum.

If anybody could help her, it was Linnette.

She stared at her friend, caught between discomfort and eagerness. "I've been sitting here fretting that you wouldn't be able to come. I know you said you didn't know how long you'd need to stay at Lady Smythe-Burke's. I do know it can be difficult to leave."

"I can see the worry upon your face, my dear. I don't know that I've ever seen you looking so flustered. Your cheeks are positively flushed—and you haven't even taken the time to compliment me on my dress. Do you know how difficult it was to find rose silk that did not clash with my carrot-colored hair? And may I say that shade of green is delightful on you. Oh dear, are you truly that upset by this silly print? You don't even smile. I can't think what else you'd need to talk to me about so urgently. I can understand why you would find being displayed in public uncomfortable, but is it truly this upsetting?"

Kathryn felt her face heat further. "You know your hair is lovely. And the dress is delicious. Forgive me for not mentioning it. I admit to being quite troubled by the print. One never does know where these things will lead, but that was not why I asked you here early. I was hoping you would come to tea again tomorrow when Annie and Elizabeth can also attend and we can talk about it then. I've even sent an invitation to the Marchioness of Tattingstong. I have another matter that I wish to discuss now."

"Nothing too troubling, I hope."

Shifting from foot to foot Kathryn fought for the words. "Nothing troubling, merely uncomfortable and perhaps embarrassing."

"Oh dear, I do hope I haven't done anything." Linnette looked her straight in the eye, as steadfast and honest as ever.

"No, it's nothing like that. I just have some questions I need answered and I don't know who else to turn to." Kathryn could only hope she was not as red as she felt. Her cheeks felt hot enough to cook griddlecakes.

"Then here I am. And forgive me for taking your place, but do you think we could perhaps be seated?" Linnette looked over at the well-cushioned settee.

Kathryn had never forgotten to offer a guest a seat in her life. Drawing in a calming breath, she gestured to a seat on the settee and took the other spot, wishing with all her heart that she knew how to begin this exchange.

Linnette reached over and took her hand. "It really cannot be that bad. Or, looking at your face, perhaps it is. Come on, out with it."

Kathryn pulled a breath deep into her lungs until it felt as if she'd pop through her corset.

One. Two. Three.

"I want to know how to please my husband." There, it was out.

Chapter Three

"You want to please your husband." Linnette spoke slowly, "Surely you know that the time to please a man is before he proposes. After the wedding it is his job to please you—or at least to ignore your shopping. Oh, don't look at me like that. I didn't realize how serious you are. You need to explain more—what do you mean by pleasing your husband, and perhaps even more importantly, why do you care? Is he acting badly towards you? Have you displeased him in some way?"

So perhaps it wasn't quite out. Kathryn wasn't even sure she had the vocabulary to describe what she needed to know. "The duke hasn't come to my bed in three months—and not often before that since—well, you can guess what since. I tried last night and he refused. He was quite polite, but he definitely refused."

"Have you ever refused him?"

"No, never. I have on occasion let him know when I was—was indisposed." This was harder than she had ever imagined. "I would never refuse him. I know my duty."

"Your duty?" Linnette appeared slightly put off by the term.

"Your duty with Robert? Oh, I am not the one you should be talking to about this."

Kathryn wasn't sure which surprised her more, Linnette referring to her husband by his Christian name, although the two had known each other from childhood—Linnette had actually introduced him to Kathryn—or Linnette not wanting to discuss marital rela . . . to discuss sex. Linnette had always had a bawdy sense of humor and seemed willing to discuss anything. It was always Kathryn who found a reason to leave the room when the conversation grew naughty. "Who else can I talk to?"

"Your mother?"

Kathryn stared back at Linnette, the ache of despair growing again in her chest.

"No, I suppose not. And not, I imagine, his mother either. Heaven forbid. One of your aunts? No, not them. Is there no other friend?"

"No one I can imagine discussing it with. I considered discussing it with Annie, but I am not sure she knows any more than me—despite having a son. Until this last year she lived at Hargrove's estate while Lord Richard stayed in Town."

Linnette leaned back and stared at the ceiling, her toe tapping. "I am still not sure that I am the right person for this."

"Why? From what I've heard, and what you've implied, you do know the answers to my questions."

"What do you mean?" Linnette sat back up and stared at her, eyes locked on her face, lips suddenly pale.

She couldn't believe this. Kathryn had never felt so mortified. Even her best friend wouldn't discuss this with her. She must be doing something really wrong. Maybe she should just let it go. "Just that, and I can't believe I am saying this, you've had several lovers since the duke died, and they always seem—well, they seemed happy, very happy."

"I cannot deny that. I have never even tried to deny it."

"Then why don't you want to help me?" She had to be brave, show courage. She had no choice. If Linnette would not help her, then there was nobody left to ask—she'd be completely alone.

Linnette leaned back again, her shoulders relaxing. "It's not that I don't want to, it's just that—Oh, never mind. Ask me anything and I will do my best to answer."

"I am not even sure what questions to ask." Kathryn glanced down at her hands. Why was this so hard? She trusted Linnette—completely.

"You mentioned duty," Linnette said slowly. "Is that really how you regard it?"

That was a hard question. In her mind she'd always thought of it as duty, but sometimes she wondered if her body wasn't seeking more. She did find it agreeable when Robert touched her. "I don't find it unpleasant."

"And does your husband know that you feel this way?"

Was she really going to have to talk about this? How was she to know what Robert thought other than that he clearly found her wanting in some way? "He knows that I don't mind it when he visits me. Sometimes I even find it pleasant. My mother told me it would be awful and I've never found it so—not even the first time. It was only a little painful."

Was that a rude noise? Kathryn glanced up at Linnette. It was impossible to tell.

There, that was definitely a sigh.

Linnette reached over and took her hand. "Do you know that many women enjoy sex—some quite a lot?"

"But surely not ladies? I've always been told that relations are for men—and for having children."

"I am sure that is what your mother told you. Do you believe that I am a lady? I have not taken those lovers that you mentioned because I needed a man as an escort. The best men in bed are always the hardest to force to attend balls and musicales. Even my first time I found pleasure—great pleasure."

"Oh." Kathryn supposed she had known this, but it was still strange to hear it put into words. Ladies enjoyed bedsport. Was it possible that she could enjoy it? She closed her eyes and tried to imagine, to imagine Robert's hands moving across her . . . and hers on him. Was she allowed to touch him? She opened her eyes as real questions finally started to form in her mind. "You found pleasure with the duke, even that first time?"

"You will find this shocking—I do not even believe I am telling you this—but the first time was not with the duke. I had a young love, a great love and with him I found true delight—even that first time."

"You—you . . . Before the duke?"

"Yes. It was a relationship that could not work at that time. He needed to leave, but it was wonderful for all of that." Linnette looked down. "And now I have hopes that it may happen again. I have become reacquainted with him and I have hopes that . . . Oh, never mind. Let us discuss your problems. That is what is of importance now." Linnette leaned forward, speaking softly. "Did Rob—your husband never try to give you pleasure?"

God, did she have to answer that? "I don't know. How would he do that?"

Linnette stared straight ahead, not looking at her. "Forgive my bluntness, but does he touch your breasts, put his hand between your legs, perhaps kiss you there?"

"His mouth there? Of course, he doesn't." That was a little too far for her to imagine.

"None of it?"

Think carefully. Take it step by step. "He touches my breasts, sometimes. He even puts his hand under my nightdress."

"Your nightdress? You wear a nightdress?"

"If it's hot, I may simply stay in my chemise." Why did Linnette seem so surprised?

"And what does your husband wear?"

"He comes into the room in his banyan."

"And then?"

"Well, he does take it off once the candle is blown out."

Linnette swallowed visibly. "Robert blows out the candle."

"Oh no. I do. My mother was most explicit on when I should do it."

"And Robert has never asked to leave it burning?"

"Why would he?"

"How old are you, Kathryn? Oh, don't answer. I know very well that you are two years younger than me, although you also came out a few years late."

"Yes. What is your point?"

"You sound like a seventeen-year-old debutante who has never even been alone in a room with a man who was not her father—not a woman married over two years."

"I know." Her voice came out as the barest squeak.

"I would have thought better of Robert."

"You confuse me again."

"It is the job of the husband to school his spouse in what he likes in the bedroom and to be sure that she also experiences pleasure."

"I often find it pleasant."

Linnette laughed, low and soft—but without malice. "There is a big difference between pleasant and pleasure."

"So there is something wrong with me."

Blowing out a long breath, Linnette answered. "I would doubt that. What I fail to understand is why Robert let this situation develop."

Kathryn thought back to the early days of her marriage. Was it possible that Robert had asked about the candle? She wasn't quite clear. The whole experience had still been quite shocking. Her father had occasionally kissed her forehead and the grooms had helped her onto her horse, but those were the only times she'd ever really been touched by men before Robert. She'd been twenty-one when she married, not the seventeen that Linnette referred to, but she'd been incredibly sheltered for all that. Her mother had never allowed her to waltz. The only dances she was allowed included little more than the brushing of hands.

"You seem suddenly lost in thought," Linnette said.

"I am just trying to consider if it could possibly be Robert's fault. I still don't see why you should think that."

"I think that because you should be having this conversation with him rather than me. He is not that frightening unless he has changed greatly in these last years."

"Have it with him? I mean, no, he is not frightening. But—but have it with him? I don't think I could do that."

"I think you may have to. If you want to please him, you will have to use words to make him understand what you want." Linnette sounded very sure.

"But I don't know what I want beyond that I want him back in my bed at night."

"And why do you want that if you only find it pleasant?"

"He needs an heir."

"Oh." That seemed to flummox Linnette for a moment, but she recovered quickly. "And is that truly the only reason?"

Kathryn allowed the question to play through her mind. Did she want Robert in her bed for reasons other than creating an heir? She stared down at her hands. Every time she thought this conversation could not grow more difficult it did. "No, I miss him. I don't know why it makes a difference in the rest of our lives, but it does. I feel like he doesn't really see me anymore. Sometimes, I think he deliberately looks anywhere but at me." She gripped Linnette's hand, which still rested on her leg. "He used to even spend the entire night in my bed. It was wonderful waking up to his smile in the morning. I felt like singing all day long."

A soft smile lit Linnette's face. "Yes, I know that feeling well. And did he seem to feel the same?"

That was harder to know. "I believe so."

"Then I think you need to work on capturing those feelings again. You say that right after your marriage he would come by regularly, but that after you lost the baby he stopped coming?"

Had Linnette really just said that? Nobody mentioned the baby, the tiny boy born months too soon. Kathryn didn't know how to respond. It felt for a moment like the heart had been ripped from her chest—and then—and then she felt fine, well, not exactly fine, but the world had not ended and life went on.

"Did I say something wrong? You look like I just ground my heel into your toe." Linnette squeezed her hand anxiously.

"No, nothing wrong. It's just that nobody ever mentions my son." It felt so good to say that, to say it out loud. "I sometimes wonder if he ever really existed, except in my mind. I mean, I know he did. I don't think I imagined the whole thing, but it feels as if he was just erased."

"Surely Robert—no, I could see that he might not. He always did have a knack for avoiding anything too unpleasant. It is often a problem with men. I wish I had known. I thought I was doing the correct thing allowing you your privacy."

"And you were out of London at the time. I believe you were seeing to the estates for the new duke until he could return from India."

"And then he never did return—and now there is another new duke." Linnette took her turn being silent. Then, forcing a smile on her face she looked straight at Kathryn. "But, let us return to your original question. You wish to seduce your husband. Is that correct?"

She'd never thought of it that way. Kathryn let the thought turn over in mind. Seduce. Seductive. Seductress. Could she be a seductress? She drew her shoulders back. "Yes, that is what I want."

"Good. It should not be difficult. Men are very easily led by a beautiful woman."

Kathryn felt herself blush again.

"Now, tell me what happened last night—when he refused you," Linnette asked.

"I saw him in the hall before dinner—his mother had just gone into the parlor. It was clear that he was heading out, not joining me in the dining room. I told him Mr. Johns had purchased some new port and that Robert could come by my room later to sample a glass."

"And?"

"And he said that he would probably have quite enough to drink while he was out and that he expected to be back late. He told me that I should not wait up."

"Hmmm. He may not have realized what you were inviting. Had you ever asked him to your room in such a manner before?"

"No. He always told me when he would visit, but he hasn't recently and so I . . ."

"I understand perfectly. I am afraid that you must be much more direct. Can you do that?"

"If—if—if I have to." Kathryn could not believe she was stuttering.

"You will need to be direct with your posture and demeanor, not just your words."

"I will manage if you tell me how."

Linnette dropped her hand and stood. "I can tell you how. I can show you how. But that will only go so far. You must believe in yourself, believe that you want your husband—and that he wants you."

What exactly did that mean? She had certainly wanted Robert as her husband, but to want him?

Walking across to the window, Linnette drew back the curtains so that the light flooded in behind her. She turned back to Kathryn and began to stroll slowly forward. Her eyes met Kathryn's and held, the barest hint of a smile turned up the corners of her mouth, her breasts pushed against the neckline of her dress which suddenly seemed inches lower than it had before, her face shone with an inner knowledge of desire, and her own desirability.

Kathryn swallowed. "How did you do that?"

"Mostly it is in the mind. I thought about my lover and what I would like to do to him, to have him do to me. And I thought about how much he wanted to do it to me, how all he desired was me."

Oh dear. "I am not sure I can do that." Kathryn dropped her gaze back to her hands. "I don't know what those feelings are like, so how can I imagine them?"

Linnette chewed on her lower lip. "It is a difficult problem." And then she smiled. "I think you do have those feelings and you just don't know it. Tell me, did Robert ever kiss you before you were married?"

"Of course."

"And did he really kiss you? Not just a peck, but a kiss in which your mouths met and sought to become one?"

"Maybe once." Kathryn looked up considering. "Right after I accepted his proposal he kissed me and he—he put his tongue in my mouth."

"And did you like it?"

"It was shocking."

"But did you like it?"

She had to be brave, to confess. "I didn't want him to stop.

I wanted him to go on, to see what would happen next. He sometimes nibbled my ear—even before we were engaged. I liked that."

"And how did your body feel, your breasts feel?" Linnette came and sat beside her again.

"I've never even thought about that, about my breasts."

"Well, think about them now. In fact that may be the secret you need. When you look at Robert and invite him to your bed, stop and think about how every inch of your body feels at that moment—and remember that kiss, that wanting more."

"I can do that." At least she thought she could.

"I am sure you can. The hard part will be that I want you to tell him. I want you to invite him to your bed and I want you tell him how you feel, physically and emotionally. Describe every tingle."

"But what if I don't tingle? What if I only feel frightened and embarrassed?"

"Then tell him that." Linnette reached over and squeezed her hand again. "Robert is a good man. If he knows you are uncomfortable, he will try and help, but you have to let him know—otherwise he may just think you cold."

"Cold is that what..."

"Enough of that. If you spend your time worrying, this will not work. I should not have said anything. Now, if your ears are ready, I have some things to say that may shock you—but you do need to listen."

Kathryn leaned forward, strangely eager to hear each detail.

Linnette hesitated, and then began, "Men like breasts—at least most men. I believe they may even love them. I have it on some authority that almost every time a man sees a woman, any woman, he wants to see her breasts."

"That cannot be true, can it?"

"I have been assured that it is—and that the woman does not even need to be attractive."

"Oh."

"So—assuming that Robert is no different, which I think is a fair statement—give him peeks at your breasts, wear something low, bend over—and when you do, when you catch his gaze falling, smile—not a big smile, but a small, mysterious one—the type of smile you give when you know a wonderful secret that nobody else knows."

Kathryn considered. "I can do that."

"I know you can. Now this may be the harder part—when you catch him looking, when you are alone, trail your fingers down your throat across your chest, draw his gaze, and hold it."

"That is not difficult."

"It may be harder than you think—and then run your finger along the top of your bodice, slip a finger underneath, let him imagine that it is him touching you, feeling you—and keep holding his glance, let him know that you are thinking the same thing, dreaming of him—let your nipples harden and think of him."

Kathryn swallowed, hard.

"And if you really want him, really want him to want you, lick your lips and leave them wet and shiny. You can even wet your finger before you touch your breasts, slip it between your lips, and..."

Oh heavens, Linnette could not just have suggested that, could she? Kathryn squeezed her legs tight and listened.

Chapter Four

Kathryn stared up at the elaborate plasterwork on the ceiling. The center medallion truly was a masterpiece, a monument to some long-dead craftsman. Her gaze dropped to the flowers on the table, a wonderful collection of cut tulips and hyacinths set in a shining crystal vase. Perfect. Even the scent was perfect. The hyacinths practically screamed of spring.

Today, however, she couldn't even pretend that she was perfect. The megrim that had taken hold of her last night, when Robert had missed dinner yet again, had made a home in her temples, her color was off—no amount of pinching her cheeks was going to bring them color. She'd done her best with her dress, or at least Mary had. The soft linen swept about her body and transformed her wan appearance into one of more delicacy.

And she had guests. The ladies were about to arrive.

The tap on the door sounded like a fist pounding. She pasted a smile on her face as Mr. Johns entered and announced Lady Richard Tennant and the Dowager Duchess of Doveshire.

"Send them in." There was no purpose in delay – and seeing Annie and Linnette would certainly improver her mood.

Even before she could finish the thought, Annie came sailing in, a grin spread across her face, her pink skirts swirling about, her dark curls bobbing in a secret wind. Linnette followed with more decorum. She shot Kathryn a questioning look and then shrugged at Kathryn's negative shake of the head.

Hurrying over, Annie took the seat beside her on the settee. Annie had not been her friend as long as Linnette, but she was still as close as a sister. Annie had come out at the same time as Kathryn, although she was a year younger, and they'd formed a bond, while worrying that nobody would ask them to dance, that could never be broken. Even Annie's quick marriage and the too soon thereafter birth of her son had not changed their relationship.

"Kathryn, you are looking well," Annie said as she spread her skirts in a pretty half circle. "That is the most wonderful shade of blue—and the lace at your cuff. Exquisite."

"Yes, Kathryn, I should have mentioned that you do look simply divine. Life must be agreeing with you." Linnette took a seat on the sofa opposite the two of them. "Are those new earrings? You always did have the best pearls."

Kathryn bit her lip, and then smiled at Annie, "Why yes, Annie, I do love blue and your gown is scrumptious. It reminds me of fresh summer raspberries. Linnette, I forgot to mention your lovely feathers when you entered. They sweep your cheek in the most becoming fashion."

Linnette grinned. "And Annie, those slippers are a masterpiece. Wherever did you get them?"

"I'll give you the direction of the shop when we leave. And Linnette, you should always wear lavender," Annie added. "It makes you look so ethereal."

"There, are we done with fashion?" Kathryn could not hold the giggle from her voice. The three of them had long ago decided that fashion and gowns and shopping were fine subjects of conversation, but only for about a minute—which wasn't to say they didn't enjoy them. A decision had been reached during Kathryn's first season that the topic would be covered quickly and then dispensed with. It had become a quiet joke between them.

A subtle joy filled her that these, her two friends, had been the first two to arrive. A few minutes in their company and all her problems would feel so much lighter. Already she was believing that she could make things work with Robert—she could always ask Linnette more questions. And as for the other matter, she might have spoken strongly with her mother-in-law, saying that there was nothing wrong with being American, but she wasn't quite sure. There certainly was nothing actually wrong with it, but would the new Lady Tattingstong possibly be comfortable within the confines of society? She'd always heard that Americans were much looser in their social mores. How did one become friends with one?

And the print? What should be made of that strange print? She'd been too busy thinking about Robert to dwell on it these last days, but it was still troubling.

Almost as if reading her mind, Linnette spoke up decisively. "If we are done with silliness, let us discuss this odd print. Who could have done it and why? We've never been together as a group and certainly not with Lady Tattingstong. Somebody must have drawn us separately and put us all together."

"Oh good, you're discussing it already—although perhaps you could have waited for me to begin." Elizabeth, the Countess of Westhampton, swept into the room. "I hope you don't mind. I told the porter I didn't need an announcement." She seated herself before Kathryn could rise, taking a chair on Kathryn's far side. That had always been Elizabeth's way—do what you want, don't wait for permission.

Kathryn had never been quite sure how she felt about the countess. She sometimes was so forceful that Kathryn felt she faded to nothing in comparison.

Linnette had no such difficulty. "If you'd been here on time, that wouldn't have been a problem."

"I arrived at the perfect time. You all arrived too early."

If either of the other women had spoken in such a fashion, Kathryn would have believed it was a joke; with Elizabeth, she was never sure.

"So do you know who is behind this hideous print?" Annie asked.

Elizabeth pulled off her gloves and dropped them on a chair. She did not even glance about to see if there was a maid to take them. "I am not sure that I find it hideous—just troubling. We must be sure it does not become a known scandal. I do prefer my scandals to be private. At least we all look quite well in it." She glanced about the room. "Is Lady Tattingstong not yet here? I understood she was also invited."

Kathryn debated for a moment, and then answered honestly. "I asked her to arrive slightly later. She will be bringing her sister, Miss Beacon. I wanted a chance for us to talk first."

"No wonder you were in a snit at my being the last to arrive. It would never have done if they had arrived first, I suppose." Elizabeth spread her skirts in a direct imitation of Annie's.

In a snit? She had not been in a snit. She hadn't even said

anything. It had been Linnette who commented. Only Elizabeth could be late and make her feel guilty. "I can't believe you approve of the print." She pulled out the copy she had saved and tossed it on the table. "They are actually selling it now. It's become—popular."

"Oh Kathryn, my dear. You can be so much like your mother. And I never said I approved. I simply do not yet disapprove." Elizabeth smiled across at her.

"I will choose to take that as a compliment. My mother was always perfectly behaved."

"I never said she was not."

Linnette leaned forward, ignoring Elizabeth. "Why don't we get this discussion moving in the correct direction before the rest of your guests arrive? Do you actually approve of the print then, Elizabeth?"

"I can't say that I approve; I just don't see it as a disaster. The drawing is flattering. There are no comments made, no hint of scandal. I just fail to see the issue. It's not like we're pictured in our chemises—or less. I actually find the whole matter kind of—of entertaining."

Kathryn pressed her lips tight. She was not even going to reply to that.

Annie picked up the conversation. "You are correct that there is nothing actually wrong with it and the artist is certainly talented. I must confess I do like the angle they've chosen for me and my hair looks quite well, but there is also nothing right about it." She lifted the print, stared at it, and then let it drift back to the table. "I merely question why it was made. As Linnette was saying when you arrived, Elizabeth, what is the purpose in putting us all together? I would understand if one or two of us were shown or it was clear we were at a real event, but why show us all together? It seems nonsensical to me. And I do admit to disliking the attention it is drawing."

There was a tap on the door, and Mr. Johns opened it to announce the arrival of Lady Tattingstong and her sister, Miss Beacon.

Kathryn felt some temptation to delay receiving them for a moment while they finished the conversation, but really what was the purpose. She nodded to Mr. Johns to direct them in.

She stood as her guests entered.

Chapter Five

They were really quite nice. Kathryn's fears faded away as she poured tea for the two Americans. Their manners were impeccable and demeanor pleasant. She didn't know what she'd been worrying about. It was clear what had drawn Tattingstong to the vibrant young woman before her. The marchioness was both beautiful and clever. Her hair was the soft blond of butter and her eyes a sweet, gentle blue. She was the very picture of an English rose—except, of course, that she wasn't.

The marchioness smiled across at her. "I'd always thought that mother did exceptionally well at teaching my sister and me how to behave properly and then I watch you pour tea and I wonder. It is such a simple thing and yet you do it with such grace and poise. Is it something you are taught or do you think it is bred into you?"

"Surely you know how to pour tea?" Kathryn answered, trying not to look at Elizabeth who was clearly rolling her eyes.

"Yes, I do. I must have poured a million cups, but I am always so conscious of each movement, of trying not to splash, of worrying whether the tea or the milk goes in the cup first."

"Why, the tea," said Linnette.

"Why, the milk," said Annie.

The marchioness laughed and her younger sister, Miss Beacon, stared at them all, wide-eyed.

"See, it is impossible," exclaimed the marchioness.

Kathryn leaned forward as if to share a great secret. "It really depends what your purpose is. You see, it is all a matter of curdling and expense."

The marchioness looked puzzled. "I am not sure that I follow."

"The tea is, of course, as I am sure we all know, the more expensive of the two liquids," Kathryn explained.

Elizabeth pursed her lips. "I am sure that I didn't know that."

Kathryn simply nodded, refusing to be childish. "If you pour the milk in first and it is not quite right, then it will curdle the moment the hot tea hits it. You will lose only a few drops of tea at most. If, however, you start with the tea, then you've wasted the whole cup, if you add milk that is not fresh. So, if you care about being frugal, you begin with the milk. If you want to show that cost does not matter, you begin with the tea."

"I never knew that," Annie said.

Linnette stood up and stretched her spine, her curves almost overflowing even the high neckline of the lavender silk. "So, have I just declared I don't care about costs? I confess that I don't—or at least not really. I do always check the housekeeping expenses, but that is mostly for form. I was never good at math and I fear time has not improved me. I always have somebody double-check my figuring on important matters."

"Well, I think that if you don't care for costs, you act more like me and just don't bother to even know the value of tea." Elizabeth rose to her feet, as if in competition with Linnette. "You expect the finest and you receive it. It can be as simple as that." She gifted Kathryn and the Lady Tattingstong with a smile that would have been better spent on an eager young buck.

Annie cleared her throat, clearly uncomfortable with the turn of the conversation. "Are we going to discuss the print or not? I am happy to continue to socialize, but I thought the purpose of our get-together was to learn who was behind this." She stabbed a finger at the print that still lay on the table where Kathryn had tossed it.

"Is that what this is about?" The marchioness raised a brow. "I had wondered at my invite."

"Of course, that's not why you were invited. I was eager to make your acquaintance and believed my friends would feel the same. We want to support you as you take your position in society." Kathryn faced Lady Tattingstong directly. "I would not wish to pretend that the print had nothing to do with the timing, but I consider it a case of friends helping friends, nothing more."

"I will accept your gesture as such," the Lady Tattingstong answered. "I must say that I know nothing about the print. I am as confused, if not more so, than any of you. To be quite honest I had to verify with my husband to be sure of all of your identities. I would have been quite incapable of designing such a thing. And assuming that the gowns you are all pictured in are as accurate as my own, more than incapable. I have only been introduced to Lady Westhampton previously. Although I will admit to having been at gatherings with both Lady Richard and the dowager duchess. It would have been impossible for me to put this together."

"Well, I certainly didn't do it," Elizabeth said. "Why on earth would I have?"

"I believe that we all feel that way," Linnette answered back, brushing a feather off her cheek and back into place.

"Why would any of us have done it?" Annie said, again trying to calm the situation.

Kathryn could only stare about at her friends. There was an edge in the air that she didn't like. She glanced between Elizabeth and Linnette. She'd heard them described as rivals but had never seen them like this before. They always bickered and picked at each other, but there was something new here. Could one of them be behind the print? It seemed unlikely that Linnette was—surely she would have told Kathryn. But, Elizabeth had never been predictable. If Kathryn had to guess, Elizabeth would have been her bet.

"Perhaps we are asking the wrong question," Miss Beacon, the marchioness's sister spoke up for the first time. She was a pretty child, blond like her sister, but with a more exotic twist. Her eyes were tilted up at the corners much like those of Kathryn's cat. It was hard to be sure if they made her more beautiful or less. Kathryn supposed it was in the view of the beholder.

"What do you mean?" Elizabeth sounded demanding rather than friendly.

Miss Beacon dropped her eyes to her steaming cup of tea. "I mean that perhaps we should try to decide why somebody drew this. It does not seem mean spirited. Perhaps whomever it is had only good intentions."

"I cannot see anything good intentioned about it," Elizabeth replied.

"But I must confess I don't see anything bad." Linnette's comment was clearly aimed at Elizabeth. The two of them seemed determined to argue no matter what viewpoint was expressed.

"Why don't you two agree to disagree?" Kathryn spoke firmly. "Fighting will serve no purpose. I think it is clear that none of us knows anything about this—or why it was done."

"Or at least not that they will admit to." Linnette stared at Elizabeth.

"Be careful," Elizabeth said straight to Linnette, ignoring the rest of them. "I am not the one with secrets."

"I am sure I don't know what you refer to," Linnette answered.

"Are any of you attending Lady Smythe-Burke's ball, later this week?" The marchioness spoke loudly. "I've heard so much about her, but must admit to being a little bit frightened. She sounds a complete terror."

Linnette sat back down, shooting a nervous look at Elizabeth. "You are quite American to be so direct, but to answer your question—she can be."

Elizabeth stayed standing, and took a step towards the Lady Tattingstong. "I don't find her so. She can be a bit forceful, but one can always sense the bit of fun in her tone. I will warn you that she does tend to ramble. It's easy not to pay attention and then find oneself asked a most important question. I know I found that the case at her last ball, a little over a week ago, wasn't it, Linnette?"

"Yes, I believe it was." Linnette did not look at Elizabeth as she spoke."

"I would have thought you would remember better." Elizabeth was glaring at Linnette. "You were having such a good time when I saw you."

Linnette did not answer.

Annie tried to step into the silence. "Only Lady Smythe-Burke would hold two such affairs in month. She is law unto herself. And yes, I am certainly planning to attend this next one. In fact, I am sure we all are." Annie smiled kindly.

Kathryn's head was spinning with the constant change of subject and emotion. She wished that Linnette and Elizabeth would just stop. She didn't know what was between them, but they didn't need to take it out on the marchioness who seemed quite nice.

The only positive note was that she was completely forgetting about her difficulties with Robert. At least she had been until now—now thoughts of yesterday's conversation with Linnette began to filter in. Could she really talk to Robert like that? Could she gaze at him and think lewd thoughts?

The idea wasn't as frightening as it should have been. In fact, she was beginning to like it.

"Well, I must be going." Elizabeth looked about for her gloves. "I have important things to do this evening."

So her tea wasn't important? Kathryn nodded to Elizabeth and rose to her feet. "Of course you do. I am sure your life must be so busy with the earl away." Oh dear, that had been catty, but sometimes it was called for.

Elizabeth turned away as if pretending she had not heard.

Linnette grinned as if Kathryn had declared sides in a

war—which had not been her intent at all. It was true that she would always choose Linnette over Elizabeth, but the last thing she wanted was a war.

The marchioness rose to her feet. Her sister followed her lead. "I am afraid we also must be going. Tattingstong does worry if I am gone too long."

"Ahh, I do remember being newly wed," Linnette added as she rose also. "And perhaps I should head off as well. I am sure you have plans to make for this evening." She shot Kathryn a knowing look.

"Don't forget both of the Dowager Duchesses of Harrington are here," Kathryn said, wishing it were not true.

"Somehow I imagine you'll manage," Linnette answered. "A determined woman is a powerful thing."

"Yes, you always were good at getting what you wanted, weren't you, Linnette?" Elizabeth was not about to let it go even as she headed to the door.

Lady Tattingstong and her sister followed in Elizabeth's wake.

"What was that about?" Annie asked, once the others were safely gone.

Linnette looked down and did not meet Annie's gaze. "Nothing, I am sure. Elizabeth is just in one of her moods."

"I don't know. It did sound like she had something particular in mind," Kathryn said.

"Please, just let it be, Kathryn." Linnette replied. "Think about your husband and our earlier discussion, not about my problems. We'll all be happier if they are simply ignored."

Chapter Six

She'd survived another dinner. Kathryn swallowed the last of her after-dinner tea and looked about her empty parlor. Robert's grandmother had gone up immediately following dinner and his mother had lasted only another fifteen minutes once it became clear that Kathryn was not going to discuss the Americans beyond reassuring the dowager duchess that the marchioness was not a savage and had not arrived in buckskins and beads. It was clear the dowager duchess had not yet heard about the print and Kathryn could only be glad. It was definitely not the type of thing one discussed with one's mother-in-law.

Placing the delicate cup back on the saucer, Kathryn looked about the room trying to decide if she should stay and wait longer to see if Robert arrived home. Normally he told her if he was going to be late and he hadn't tonight. Missing dinner was the only thing he'd mentioned.

She couldn't wait until the Season started in a few weeks. Sitting and waiting was not something she was good at. Her nerves were stretched tighter than a kite string. If she wasn't careful, she would snap.

How was she ever going to seduce her husband? Even the

thought had her shivering—and only partly with pleasure. She closed her eyes and imagined him entering the room, imagined standing and walking toward him, imagined her shoulders pulled back, her breasts pressed tight against her dress. She would step forward slowly, letting her hips sway. Stopping just before she reached him she'd . . .

She didn't know what she'd do.

Robert's brandy sat in a decanter at the corner of the table near her elbow, a selection of glassware about it. She'd never had more than a sip, and that medicinally. Now, however, the thought of a full glass drew her.

With hands that shook only slightly she grasped the decanter and poured. The first swallow burned, the second warmed, the third soothed. Sipping from the glass, she reclined in her seat and began imagining again. . . .

She would step forward slowly, letting her hips sway. Stopping just before she reached him, she'd tilt her lips up, lean a little forward . . .

Her mind stopped again. She could get so close, could feel his breath in her hair and then—she just didn't know. She should have asked Linnette more questions.

Did she kiss him? Was that too forward? Might he be disgusted by unladylike behavior?

Why hadn't she ever tried anything before?

Another large swallow of brandy—and another.

Yes, she would kiss him, would feel the bristles on his chin beneath her lips, would taste the salt of his skin, inhale the deep musk of his scent. Her lips would move over the curves of his cheeks, edging ever closer to his mouth. She'd know he wanted her kiss and she'd wait, she'd tease, she'd . . .

Well, that was better. She'd made it much further before becoming flummoxed.

Downing the rest of the glass, she poured another.

Now she could imagine her fingers tangled in his hair, the soft dark waves velvet beneath her touch. She'd pull his head closer, feel the heat of his breath beneath her chin—lower. She'd slip her hands down, pull at his cravat, letting her fingers feel the strength of his neck—her lips following . . .

"I've never seen you drink brandy before." Robert's voice sounded from the door.

Her gaze rose, taking in his rumpled attire, his broad shoulders and lean hips—and those lips. Her eyes slowly moved up until they locked on his mouth, the mouth she'd just been dreaming about, imagining. His lips were firmer in reality, but fuller too. So inviting . . .

"How many glasses have you had? I've never seen quite that look upon your face." He stepped into the room, moved toward her, his own gaze intent upon her face.

"This is only my second. I haven't quite decided if I like it." She took another sip, her lips curving about the now warm glass, her tongue darting out to taste.

His whole focus seemed to sharpen. She wasn't sure he saw anything except the tiny spot where her mouth and the brandy met. She dipped her tongue in again.

He chest rose and fell quite noticeably. Why had she never considered his response to her actions before?

She licked the rim.

He took two steps forward.

Lowering the glass, she ran her tongue about her lips, tasting for each remaining bit of heat. "I think I may be beginning to like it quite a bit. How would you feel about having a wife with a penchant for brandy?"

His gaze rose, his eyes full of heat and intensity. "I think I could become accustomed to it."

Oh dear. She swallowed, took a quick gulp of brandy. A part of her wanted to flee, a part of her wanted to welcome him into her arms—most of her didn't know what to do. She stared up at him, unsure.

Watched him take another step forward.

"You're home earlier than usual tonight." Did her voice shake? She knew her hands were.

"I didn't say I'd be particularly late—just that I wouldn't attend dinner."

"No, you didn't." Yes, her voice was definitely not steady. Her gaze dropped to her hands and she pulled it back up. She would not back down now.

"How was tea this afternoon?" He moved so only an arm's length remained between them.

She could feel the heat of his body, sense his movement in the air. "Tea?"

"You did meet with Tattingstong's wife, did you not?"

"Oh yes, of course." How could he be thinking at all when the air sizzled between them? She felt her own breaths grow shallow.

"And how did you find her?" He reached out and traced a curl that brushed her cheek.

"Quite lovely, actually." It felt like all the breath had been sucked from her chest.

"I am glad. He deserves a good wife."

Something in his tone caught her, said so much more than

the words. "Don't all men deserve a good wife?" She clasped his hand between hers and rose to standing.

"I would imagine that there are many men who most definitely do not deserve a good wife," he replied.

She pulled his hand to her lips, breathing deeply against it.

He continued, "I always thought I deserved one. This last year or more I have not been so sure."

She placed a soft kiss against his fingertips. "I am quite sure you deserve a good wife."

"Even after . . ." He hesitated and she was not sure what he meant to say.

She waited—not wanting to risk a mistake. This moment was too important.

Instead of saying more he opened his hand and stroked her cheek softly. "And you, my dear duchess, do you deserve a good husband?"

"I try to." She stared straight into his eyes. "I am not always sure I succeed."

"Isn't that for me to judge?" His gaze dropped from her eyes to her lips, almost tangible, an invisible caress.

Should she kiss him? Every ounce of her wanted to lean up on her toes and lay her lips against his, to feel the firm movement of his mouth. It would be so easy.

Her feet started to lift, but she hesitated. What if she did it wrong?

There had been that one wonderful kiss right after their engagement and a few more after the wedding, only Robert had always led. But tonight was about her seducing him.

She reached up, her whole focus on his mouth, his wonderful delectable mouth. She grew almost dizzy as she moved toward her desire.

She swayed.

He caught her.

"How many brandies did you say you'd had?" he asked.

"Only two—but there was wine with dinner."

"And how many glasses did you partake in?"

"Your mother and grandmother were both present for the meal."

"Ahh, so more than you should have." He laid a hand on each of her shoulders. "Was my mother very difficult?"

"No more than usual."

"So yes, she was. I am sorry. I should not be leaving her to you. It is just that I have been so busy." He did not look at all repentant.

"She does seem to want to discuss something with you. She keeps asking when you will be joining us. If you did not want her here, why did you agree to the visit?"

Robert stepped back, but did not remove his hands. "I am not sure I did. My mother never asks. She just does. Do you really wish to discuss this now?" He suddenly looked very weary.

"No. I was thinking that perhaps it was time to retire." She took a step away, his hands slipped from her shoulders. Her legs wobbled only slightly. "Perhaps you'd like to try that port I mentioned last night."

"I don't think you need another drink."

"But perhaps you'd like a taste. I've been told it is very sweet on the lips."

The room tilted as she turned and walked toward the door. Perhaps she'd had more wine with dinner than was wise—and then the brandy. She did feel delightfully warm inside, however. And not at all embarrassed by what she was planning.

With great determination she exited the parlor and made her way to the stairs. They did seem much longer than usual, but she would manage.

The reward would be worth it.

Port? Nothing could be sweeter than Kathryn's lips. Robert watched the slow sway of her hips as she preceded him from the room. Tilting a bit, she righted herself with a hand on door. Clearly, she'd imbibed a bit more than she should.

Should it matter?

Did it matter?

It had been months since he'd shared her bed, months since he'd shared any bed. His deprivation was his own fault. While he'd desired her—he desired her always—the thought of her coming to him out of duty and nothing more had continued to eat at him. When he looked at her, it was hard to overcome his guilt and fear of another pregnancy.

It hurt so much to have lost their son. The thought of possibly losing her also was unbearable.

She took another step, reached the stairs, placed a hand on the railing, and began a slow ascent. Again, his eyes were drawn to her hips, so soft, so round—so everything he'd always wanted.

Without thought, he began to follow, his mind blanking of everything but want.

She was his wife. She was his. Why was he bothering with all these questions?

There was only one answer.

He reached the bottom stair with speed, his eyes level with her buttocks. His hands rose as if to reach out and grab. She was his wife, but the stairs were not the place.

Patience. Patience. Only a moment more.

The first stair creaked as he trod upon it and her head turned, a slow smile upon her lips.

He didn't think he'd ever seen that expression of want and seduction upon her face before. Maybe he should have plied her with brandy long ago—or port.

Had she been inviting him to her bed last night when she'd offered him a taste? Had his own desire blinded him to hers?

He moved up the stairs quickly, drawing almost even as they reached the hall at the top.

She stopped there, reached out, and laid a hand upon his chest.

Strangely, it was one of the first times he could remember her reaching for him, touching him.

Something in his chest, his heart, tightened and held.

The warmth of her fingers penetrated the linen of his shirt, sending flashes of passion through him. Her hand, so small against his chest, stroked softly, her eyes alight with wonder as if experiencing touch for the first time.

"I can feel your heart," she said, her eyes rising to meet his.

He wondered if she could feel it stop at her words—and then start again, its beat increasing by the second. He placed his one of his own hands over hers, holding it there, tight—afraid to let her go, to let this moment go.

Her smile widened then, spreading wide across her face. "I am better at this than I ever thought."

He shook his head, trying to clear the enchantment, to take meaning from her words. "Better at what?"

"At seducing you." Her smile grew to a full grin. She stepped back, and, still watching him, moved in the direction of her room. "Give me a moment and then you can join me for—for that glass of port."

She walked into the room, shutting the door all but a crack. He almost followed immediately, but she had asked for a moment.

He looked at the paintings on the wall, his ancestors from generations back. He looked at the rich carpets, the well-polished wood of the stair rail, the fine brocaded wallpaper that his mother had hung a generation ago. He'd never felt so pleased with his home, with his life, with . . .

Almost as if conjured by his thought, a voice trailed down the hall, and not the voice he wished. "Harrington, is that you? Harrington?" His mother spoke in as loud a whisper as her sense of propriety would allow.

He thought about running—or ducking into Kathryn's room to hide. Only the fear that his mother would follow stopped him. He didn't know exactly what Kathryn was using her moment for, but he'd hate to have his mother barge in and embarrass her.

"Yes, mother," he answered.

Her door opened and she stepped into the hallway, enveloped in deep purple velvet. God, where had that robe come from? Her hair hung in a silver braid over her shoulder. "Harrington, I've been meaning to speak to you."

"So my wife informed me."

"Then why haven't you sought me out?" She glared at him, her eyes shining in the light of the candelabra that lit the hall.

"I imagined that you had retired for the night."

"That is no excuse."

"I am here now. What did you wish to discuss that required you to appear in the hall unclothed?" That last bit was intended solely for her benefit. He wouldn't have cared if she'd walked down the halls naked—as long as he was far, far away. He pushed his mind from the thought.

"I understand that you've been having conversations with that woman again."

"That woman?" he asked, although he knew exactly whom she meant. She'd feuded with Linnette since Linnette had been little more than a child. And when Linnette had married and come to live at the neighboring estate, the clash had grown monumental. His mother was convinced that Linnette had had the trees along the lane cut back just so that his mother's complexion would freckle.

"Her Grace of Doveshire—although I hesitate to use the title—I've never known a woman less worthy of it."

"Yes, I've been in discussion with her. We've been discussing the possibility of a canal."

"A canal? Why on earth would you be discussing a canal? We've never had a canal."

And therefore they should never have one? Robert knew exactly how his mother thought. Never mind that a generation ago there had not been the huge demand for coal that the new industrialization had developed. "I am just considering the matter. A railroad may make more sense. I think we are already too late for a canal."

"And why are you talking to that woman about it?"

"I must. The path runs across Doveshire. With no duke in residence, it only made sense to speak to her grace." He thought back to a conversation he had earlier that day with Mr. Swatts. Swatts was apparently a distant cousin of both the new and old dukes and had held some hopes of inheriting himself. He had not sounded at all pleased when he told Robert that the new duke had apparently arrived over a week ago., If it was true it would only make everything more complicated – and Robert felt no need to share any of that with his mother.

"Hmm, I am not sure that I agree—and it does cause talk. If even I've heard rumors, then I can only imagine who else is talking of it."

He personally thought that his mother heard things before anyone else in London, but he was not going to say anything. "Do we need to discuss this now? I promise that I will find you in the morning."

"Fine." She did not sound fine. "Just remember, if I am hearing talk, then your wife will too, and that is no way to begin producing that heir you're being so slow about. And from what I hear, the new duke has arrived. You can talk to him if you really want to waste our money on canals and trains. Good night."

He should have known that his mother would know of the new duke. Robert noticed she did not add "sleep well." But then, sleep was the last thing on his mind.

He waited until his mother's door closed with a decisive

click and then turned back to Kathryn's chamber. His whole body tensed with pleasure at the thought of what was to come.

"Harrington . . . Oh, Harrington . . ."

Damnation. Not his grandmother too!

He turned, schooling his face to a neutral expression, although he wasn't sure his grandmother would see his features clearly in the dim light. "Yes, your grace?"

"Harrington, what are you doing about at this hour? Don't you know all decent men are in their beds?" His grandmother stepped into the hall, a nightshirt of thick white linen wafting about her.

"I was just heading in that direction." His door was just past Kathryn's, a step in that direction moved him closer to both.

"Then why were you talking? It's a bad habit to speak with oneself. There will be rumors that you are not quite right."

"My mother was here a moment ago."

"And what did she have to say? Nothing sensible, I am sure. I don't know why you'd be holding a discussion with her at this hour in the hall. The young have no sense." Not waiting for a reply she returned to her room mumbling. He noticed she did not close her door fully. Was she waiting to catch him committing some prank in the hall?

He waited one more moment for stillness to settle over the hall. He glanced at the still glowing candles, stepped forward, and blew them out—he didn't need a footman or some hallboy wandering this night.

Two steps to Kathryn's room, in the darkness the thin line of light under her door drew him invitingly. The handle turned quietly beneath his hand. Pushing the door open, he stepped in . . . and beheld the most beautiful, unwelcoming sight he had ever seen. His wife lay sprawled across the bed, her gown loose about her shoulders, the delicate lace of her chemise poking through. Her hair spread wondrously, in dark satin waves across the pillows, her delicate ears peeking out, her cherry lips pursed as if inviting his kiss – a faint purr escaping from them.

Even as he watched she stretched slightly, and then curled forward, a young kitten making herself comfortable.

His already tense body strained in desire as he stared at that mouth, enjoyed the curve of her body, remembered all his unfulfilled carnal fantasies.

Fantasies that would remain unfulfilled for yet one more night.

Her eyes lay shut, the dark lashes shadows upon her cheeks.

And as if that were not message enough, that delicate purr was in truth an unmistakable snore.

He turned away, willed his unruly body to relax, dreaded the sleepless night that was to come.

And turned back again, shedding coat and shirt, dropping his trousers as he walked to the bed.

Unfulfilled tonight, yes — but there was always morning.

It was time he taught his duchess the true glory of morning.

The Maids

"Look there's another one," Abby said excitedly, as she rushed over to the apothecary's window. "There are only three of them pictured this time and I can't remember who is who. Come tell me."

With little pretext of disinterest, Jane walked up to the window. The first morning light was glinting down the street and reflected brightly off the glass. She had to squint to see.

"Oh, they're at tea. I do feel like I am getting a sneak glance in at their lives." Jane pushed her nose almost to the glass to see through it. "The one in the middle is the Duchess of Harrington again—where Mary is employed. Mary did say something about them all coming to tea. I believe the Dowager Duchess of Harrington, the younger, was quite upset. She did not approve of having the Marchioness of Tattingstong and her sister to the house. The duchess, herself, apparently held no such views."

"Who are the other two? I don't see the marchioness in the print—neither of the other two have those bosoms and I don't see an American flag anywhere."

Jane stepped back. The light had shifted just enough that

she could gain better perspective. "I am trying to remember what Mary said. I think this one," she pointed at the standing woman on the left, "is the Countess of Westhampton. She's the one whose husband took off to some tropical island a month after the wedding and hasn't been back since. Don't you remember all the gossip at the time? The footmen were wondering if he'd even found her bed. I never did figure out if they were poking fun at her or at the earl."

"I thought she was supposed to be a little mouse—a country cousin or something. She does not look like a mouse."

Jane examined the drawing of the fine-boned woman, shoulders straight, sleek, dark hair smoothed back, with no allowance for fashionable curls. No, she did not look like a mouse. She looked ready for anything. Jane could almost picture her slanted, dark eyes flashing, that strange half-smile parting her lips, as she commanded an army. She was beautiful, incredibly so, but her sense of command was even stronger. A man would be a fool to get in her way—perhaps that was why the earl had fled to . . . Jane couldn't remember where, but she wasn't sure it was warm and tropical—although it was southern. "Maybe she's changed. I do remember hearing that she was a quiet thing."

"Maybe it's not her—maybe it's one of the other duchesses."

"No, I am sure it's her."

"Then who is that sitting next to the Duchess of Harrington? She looks like she could be quiet. I can't figure who she is."

"No, I think that's Lady Richard Tennant. She's not a duchess, but if her husband's older brother doesn't get busy and find a wife, her son will be a duke."

"I've never even heard of her. Why is she with the others?"

"I believe she was a childhood friend of Her Grace of Harrington. She, Lady Richard, has been in the country since just after her wedding a few years ago. Mary said that her husband didn't want her in London and she came anyway."

"Why wouldn't her husband want her here? She is very pretty."

Lady Richard's appearance was much more reserved than either of the other two women in the print, but in some ways Jane thought she would be the most fun to talk to, there was something in her little grin and dancing eyes that spoke of kindness and fun. "I do like her curls. I wonder how long it takes her maid to create them?"

Abby leaned toward the window. "I bet they're really hers. She doesn't look like she needs more than a couple of rag ties to put them in order."

"You could be right. I do wonder why it's only the three of them. Mary said six of them were at tea, and the marchioness brought her sister, although one hardly noticed the little American girl. Mary said the parlor maid said she didn't say more than two words."

"The print does make me feel like I am right in the room with them. Maybe that's why there are only three—the artist was trying to make it seem real."

"Well, he certainly succeeded. Like I said before, I feel like I am peeking in on some secret meeting."

"I don't think it's secret at all. I think they're just having a wonderful time—although, look how the countess is glaring at someone off the paper. I wonder who has her so angry?"

Chapter Seven

Kathryn couldn't ever remember feeling so warm and toasty—although her mouth felt quite dry. For the briefest of moments she lay back in bed and enjoyed, only gradually becoming aware of the warm body cuddled against her own. Turning toward the warmth she shifted and instantly a thousand needles sliced into her brain—and then her belly.

She rolled from the bed frantically, reaching for the bowl on the washstand. She clutched the basin, the china cold beneath her fingers and prayed for mercy as the remains of last night's dinner left her. It felt like she was dying—and if she wasn't, she wanted to.

She knelt on the bare boards of the floor as wave after wave of nausea swept through her, emptying her until there was nothing left. She hadn't felt this miserable since the first months of her pregnancy.

The thought left her cold. Her head had not ached like this then, but the nausea had been the same, the same desperate surge from bed in the morning, leaving behind her husband's warm body—

Robert was in her bed. She didn't remember much of the end of last night, but Robert was in her bed.

Her head jerked up, pain shooting in all directions and she met his dark gaze, his eyes tracing her features to the mess of slop in the bowl. His glance dropped away and she could see the strain and pain in his features.

She swallowed, fighting back the bile that threatened to rise again in her throat.

He, too, was remembering those mornings, early in their marriage, when she'd tumbled from bed to the basin. He too was remembering the cause—and the outcome.

There should be something to say. Maybe if her mind had not been so blurred by pain and fatigue, she could have found words, but all that she had were feelings, bleak, miserable feelings.

Ignoring the pain she pushed to her feet, going to call for the maid to take the bowl away. All would be better when it was gone.

There was a tap at the door, the maid entered without comment—and left.

All was not better.

The air was a trifle clearer, but that was all.

Slowly she turned to face her husband, her mind still searching for the words that must be there. "I am sorry. This was not what I had intended. I only—"

"Then perhaps you should not drink more than you can handle." His voice was sharp, his features cold, before he turned his body away from her.

Kathryn was glad she was still in, or at least mostly in, her dress from the night before. She would have felt horribly exposed with him glaring at her like that if she'd had only thin linen about her.

She wrapped her arms about her breasts, hugging the slipping neckline closer. "I said I was sorry."

"I am sorry, too." That sounded a bit kinder.

"I didn't know the brandy would be so strong."

"Couldn't you taste the burn? Don't you know anything?" Perhaps not kinder, after all.

Did he mean to be so cruel? She wrapped her arms tighter. "No, evidently I don't know anything—not anything at all." She would have killed for a glass of water, but could not bear to have the maid witness this interaction—perhaps she could drink the wash water. It was clean. She had not touched the pitcher when she'd grabbed for the basin.

Robert shifted on the bed, moving to sit, the sheets held loosely, but carefully to his waist. What was he afraid of? Did he think she would expect him to service her now? She felt another wave of nausea, but held it back. The maid had taken the bowl with her.

Turning towards the table and pitcher, and away from her husband, she dipped her fingers in the cool water, splashing it over her face and down her neck.

Did she have to be so damn beautiful? Did his morning cockstand have to drive all thought from his brain, to make him brusque? Did he have to wound her further every time he opened his mouth? The water ran down her neck, drawing his eyes to the faint curve of her breasts visible above her clenched arms.

His body responded again—it was morning. Dammit. He pulled the sheet higher, being careful to drape it appropriately. She was pale enough without being confronted with that.

How could he look at her, standing there so pale and sick, and think only of what he wanted, craved? Kathryn looked like she wished she could die and all he could think of was how warm she'd been in the bed with her buttocks cuddled against him, how delicious she looked in the morning light, of how he'd like to loosen her fingers, to slide the dress down, to bury his face between her breasts . . .

Bloody hell, he needed to be thinking about dry toast and tea, not fucking his wife. He added the vulgarity deliberately, trying to shock himself to reason. It didn't work. He shifted, even more uncomfortably. His body took the thought—and the word—all too literally.

Dry toast and tea.

That what was she'd called for back when—for the first time, his mind put it all together—back when his child had been in her belly, back when she'd been violently ill each morning and then looked at him with the biggest grin on her face, her eyes sparkling with joy. Her look had proclaimed that the world could not be a better place.

His arousal diminished. She'd been happy back then and all he'd been able to think of was that he couldn't have sex if she was vomiting. What an inconsiderate lout he'd been.

He still was—his erection might not be straining, but it was refusing to leave.

"I am so sorry," her quiet continued apologies, drew his eyes to her face, her pallid, unhappy face. She didn't look happy now. It might not have been possible for her to look more dejected.

"I did not mean to speak harshly. I was taking my own frustrations out on you. It was not the morning I had planned." He'd have left if he could. Was it possible to walk out with an entire sheet wrapped about his waist? Was there any way to untangle it from the bed without giving her a full display? Dammit, where were his trousers?

Shit, they were over by the door. He should have been sure they were near the bed—not that this scenario had presented itself as a possibility when he'd climbed into bed the previous evening. "Would you fetch me my trousers?" He pointed over to them where they lay, legs still tangled and half inside out.

She walked over slowly, as if afraid she'd break if she moved with vigor. She lost even more color as she bent and picked them up, but regained it when she was upright once again.

"It helps if you drink something," he said, looking about her chamber for a glass. The decanter of port stood on a table by the fireplace, two cut-crystal glasses beside it.

Grabbing his pants from her, he shimmied into them as decorously as he could. He noted that she looked pointedly away. Couldn't she even bear to look at him? Did his lack of desirability extend that far?

Standing, he walked over and grabbed a glass.

"No, please—I don't want a drink." Her eyes were glued to the port.

"I was just getting you some water, if you don't mind drinking your unused wash water."

"Oh." She held out her hand eagerly as he approached with the water.

"Would you like tea and toast? I can have your maid fetch some."

Why did that make her pale even further? What was wrong with tea and toast? It was what she always had when she was nauseous in the morning.

"Tea would be nice. I don't think I can handle toast, my stomach is roiling."

"But you always have toast when . . ."

"That was different." She looked down at the floor. "There is a great difference between being with child and overindulging."

Could the room have been more silent? He could hear the wind blowing through the window, the faint tread of feet far down the hall, the sound of a maid whistling softly—all noises he never even realized were there.

What he could not do was think of a single word to say. They'd already said "I am sorry" far too many times this morning.

"Why can you never talk of him?" Her head rose, her eyes staring into him, through him.

"Him?"

"Our son. Why do you never mention our son?"

Again, there were no words. His son. Their son. What good were words against pain? "I thought that you would not want to. The physician said that it was better to just get past it."

"And how does one get past something like that? Do you think ignoring it helps?"

She was expecting an answer, demanding an answer.

"I only did what was suggested," he replied.

Her shoulders slumped, her dress slipping slightly lower. His eyes were drawn to the lush roundness of her breasts, but thankfully his body was beyond response.

She turned away and walked across the room to stare out the window. "I always thought this view was perfect. When you first brought me here, I thought that nothing could be more beautiful."

"I agree." He was not looking at the window.

"I almost never look out now."

Did that mean she felt trapped? Had he trapped her here, here in this ice blue chamber?

"I spent too many hours imagining playing on the grass with our child—our children. Even now, when I look out, I see them there, a little girl in fluttering skirts, a toddling boy chasing a ball—and a puppy. I don't know why, but there is always a puppy. I've never even had a dog."

A puppy. He would get her a puppy. He'd never even thought of that. A puppy would make her happy. Who wouldn't smile if they had a puppy?

Oh, he knew it was not really the answer, but surely a puppy could only help.

She turned back from the window. "I need to call my maid. I may have ruined this dress already. It was not made for sleep. I couldn't get out of it without help—and then I fell asleep."

"Waiting for me." He almost offered to help, but didn't trust himself. If his fingers brushed against her skin, her breasts, her . . . Sometimes he hated being a man, hated how instantly his thoughts could—

"Yes." Her shoulders rose again. She bit her lip, drew in a deep breath and . . . "I was so proud of myself for seducing you and . . ."

She'd never seen him turn that color before. Could a man both lose all his color and turn a shade of eggplant at the same time?

"You were what?" It sounded like the words came from deep within his chest.

Did she have to say it again? It had taken all her courage to say it once. Did he not believe her? She wished she'd had the ability to add one of Linnette's knowing little looks, but that was too much to ask, given that knives were still piercing her skull. "I was proud I had seduced you, that you wanted to come to my bed."

"You seduce me?"

Did he have to sound so baffled by the words? She was sure she'd implied something similar last night. She wasn't sure whether to scream, to hit him—or to cry her heart out.

"You thought you needed to seduce me? When have you ever needed to seduce me?"

He was too much. "When have you ever not come to my bed for three months? What am I supposed to do?"

"You thought you needed to seduce me?"

Did he have to keep repeating that phrase? "Well, you didn't come when I just asked."

"When did you ask?"

"The other night—I asked you to come for port."

"You meant you wanted me to come and have se— to come to your bed?"

"Yes, dammit. I meant for you to come to my bed." She'd just cursed. He had driven her to curse. She'd have done it again if the room had not begun to slowly revolve. She took a step back toward the bed.

"Well, why didn't you say so? I am always happy to oblige." He grinned, he actually grinned.

She was going to kill him, if she didn't die first. "Well, why haven't you come to my bed in months then? You do want to have an heir, don't you?"

His grin faded. "This is about having a baby? You want to try again?"

"Of course, I do. It's my duty to give you an heir."

He turned and looked at the empty fireplace. He still stood upright, but somehow he seemed crumpled. "I will attend to you tonight then. Forgive me if I leave now. You look like you could use more rest. I will send the maid with tea—and perhaps a hot bath. A hot bath is always good."

Robert pivoted and strode towards the door.

How had everything gone so wrong so quickly? She felt like she'd kicked his—oh, what the hell—his balls. What had she said to do that to him? One moment he'd seemed excited, if baffled, by the idea of her as a seductress and then—something Linnette had said came back to her.

"Robert."

He paused, his hand on the door handle.

She could do this.

"Robert, it's not just that I want a baby, want to give you an heir. I want—I don't actually know what it is that I do want. I was hoping you could teach me."

He stood still for a moment, his back frozen straight. His head turned, and he stared at her, his face unreadable.

Then he opened the door slowly.

Had she lost?

"I will send for the tea and a bath." He stepped forward. "And Kathryn, assuming you are feeling better, perhaps you could invite me for that glass of port this evening."

Chapter Eight

Kathryn stared up at the elegant brick house. She hadn't wanted to come, but in the end had decided it was necessary to discuss the second print—and far better than sitting home and thinking about tonight. If she thought about it anymore, she'd become deranged.

Tonight was the night. She'd been invited to seduce her husband—and to have him teach her all she wanted to know.

Her toes curled within her shoes. She was thrilled.

She was terrified.

Could she really do it?

"Well, are you going to go in?" Linnette walked up behind her. "It is a beautiful house and the gardens are spectacular for this time of year, but I am not sure it's worthy of such intense scrutiny."

"Do you think the marchioness planned the gardens? I don't remember ever admiring them before. What are those wonderful fuchsia flowers in the planters at the corner? They do look like a woman must be responsible."

"So have we moved from idle chatter about fashion to flowers?" Linnette slipped an arm through Kathryn's and started to lead her toward the door. "I've never heard you chatter in such a manner."

Kathryn slowed to a crawl. "I am going to do it tonight."

"Do it?" Linnette hesitated, then swung and faced her. "Do you mean do it as in the 'it' it?"

"I mean it as in seduce my husband. I am going to be a seductress." Just saying the words gave her hope and joy. Could you dance on a stranger's walkway?

"I am glad." Linnette squeezed her hand. "I have always wanted you to be happy, Kathryn. Whatever else, do believe that."

"Of course." Why would Linnette even feel the need to say such a thing? They would be friends forever.

"We should go in."

"Yes." Kathryn stepped towards the door. The sooner this was done with, the sooner she could be home—with Robert. She could only hope that his mother would be out late at the musical evening she planned to attend.

The door swung open as they approached, a liveried footman waiting. "Lady Tattingstong is waiting in the back garden." The footman led the way through the house.

The back garden? That was odd, but perhaps it was an American custom. Surely it was more appropriate to receive guests for the first time in the parlor or a sitting room?

Still, as the glass conservatory doors swung open, Kathryn had to admit it was lovely. The day could not have been more lovely and the marchioness clearly had a way with flowers. The small walled enclosure was a veritable rainbow of blooms.

The marchioness stood as they entered, a wide smile spreading naturally across her face. "I am so pleased you could make it. I know that this second print is probably of no more importance than the first, but it seems so strange that it is so like our first meeting. I know that I am not in it, but still I find it disconcerting. I felt it was necessary for us to meet and discuss it. It could almost have been drawn from life."

Kathryn stepped forward, finding that her own smile matched the marchioness's. "First, let me say, Lady Tattingstong, that your gardens are delightful. You will have to tell me your secret. But, yes, it is odd. I think that even our sitting positions were correct. I must assure you that I did question my staff and they all deny any knowledge—and we have nobody of recent employment in the house. Well, there is my personal maid, but she would have no more knowledge of how we were seated than a stranger on the street."

"Please make yourself comfortable." Lady Tattingstong gestured to a delicate cast-iron table and chairs. "I've sent for lemonade, but can have tea brought if you prefer. I thought the day just called for lemonade."

"That sounds wonderful," Linnette answered and Kathryn nodded her agreement.

They took their seats as the marchioness's sister, Miss Beacon wandered out and, after a quick greeting, took a chair slightly removed from the others, her soft gold hair glinted in the sunlight and Kathryn was caught by how young and fresh she appeared. Kathryn could not remember ever feeling that young.

"Am I late?" Annie came rushing into the garden, her face flushed. "I do apologize." She turned to the marchioness and made all the proper greetings. After a moment, she came and sat between Kathryn and Linnette. "I've just dined with Lord

Richard. We actually spoke. I think more might have been said if Hargrove hadn't arrived. He has agreed I can stay in Town." She spoke very quietly, almost a whisper. Clearly she did not wish her voice to carry to the Americans.

"I am pleased for you," Kathryn replied equally softly, her toes almost tapping as she considered how wonderful it could be to reconcile with one's husband—not that she and Robert had ever actually argued.

Linnette brushed an imagined wrinkle from her skirt, and spoke up so that their hostess could hear. "I must say you do look delightful, Lady Richard. Is that a new brooch? I've never seen that combination of turquoise and topaz. The topaz almost matches your eyes. Did your husband give it to you?"

"No, his brother the Duke of Hargrove." Annie nodded at Lady Tattingstong. "Hargrove always sends me a gift on my son's birthday. I think he is pleased that he does not need to worry about an heir." She turned back to Linnette. "And let me say that shade of fern green is incredible. It shows off your hair most becomingly."

"You mean it doesn't make me look like I've begun to rust on top?"

"Oh, stop it, Linnette. You know very well that your hair is beautiful. I don't know why you persist in the self-deprecation." Annie studied Kathryn. "And you look beyond compare. I know I've seen that dress before, that robin's egg blue is unmistakable, but there is something about you." She allowed her gaze to sweep Kathryn from her toes to the crown of her head. "Your pearls do add a glow to your skin—I think I would wear them every day if they were mine, but that is not it. Oh, I don't know what it is, you look exactly the same and yet different."

Kathryn peeked at Linnette and couldn't suppress a small grin. She knew exactly what the difference was—she felt hope. She was going to be a seductress. Even the word caused a small tingle to begin in her belly.

"And Lady Tattingstong, let me commend you on that shade of crimson. I would never have considered it a daytime color, but on you it is perfection. Oh dear, I did not mean that to sound sarcastic. Did it? I truly think you look lovely. I was not trying to cast any aspersions upon your taste. I truly do admire your brave choice. I am only making it worse, aren't I? I never do well when I ramble." Annie clamped her lips shut.

Linnette leaned forward, toward Lady Tattingstong. "Perhaps I should explain. It is a kind of game that we play, discussing fashion. As it must be done—and we do enjoy it—we try to get it over with all in a rush at the start."

"Oh." Lady Tattingstong did not look convinced.

"It is true," Kathryn added her voice to the discussion. "It began the first season that I came out. Everywhere we went the only thing the other girls discussed was bonnets and slippers."

"That's not quite true—they did discuss men," Linnette added.

"You would mention men," Annie said, and then closed her lips again.

"I do know you didn't mean that the way it sounded, Annie," Linnette spoke up.

Lady Tattingstong was looking quite confused. "I did not realize you had been friends so long."

"Perhaps you can join us in our game," Kathryn said. "Annie is correct, you do have wonderful fashion sense—or perhaps it is your sense of colors. You're garden does show the same flair."

"Play your game with you?" Lady Tattingstong considered for a moment. "I think I would like that very much, but only if you call me Annabelle. I cannot help but see that you often use Christian names, and it would make me feel quite included if you would do the same."

"Of course," Annie spoke up, clearly eager to cover any worry that her words had been taken wrong.

"And you must call me Lucille, Lady Ric—" Annabelle's sister said. Kathryn had almost forgotten her existence.

They really should talk about the print so that she could get home. Kathryn wasn't exactly sure what preparations were necessary for seduction, but she would dearly love another bath to soothe her nerves. She opened her mouth to reintroduce the subject, when Elizabeth came hurrying in.

"How could you?" Elizabeth walked right up to Linnette and began waving a sheet of paper in her face. "I know you are never happy unless every man in the room is after you, but this is a step too far. What you did to me was bad enough. This—this—this is unthinkable."

Kathryn could only stare. She'd never seen Elizabeth in such high color. With her straight frame and high cheekbones she'd always looked like a warrior queen, but now she looked ready to cut down a nation singlehandedly.

"I don't know what you are talking about." Linnette kept her voice calm. "We've all seen the print already, as you well know. It is what we are here to discuss."

"I don't believe you've seen this print." Elizabeth waved the paper again. "I saw them pasting it in the window when I was on my way here. I cannot believe you've done this, that you think you'll get away with it."

Annie, the peacemaker as always, tried to calm the situation. "Really, Elizabeth, why don't you have a seat and a nice glass of lemonade? I am sure that you could use something cold. You look like you've run all the way here."

"Yes, why don't you have a drink and then you can tell us what has you so bothered. Does it help us figure out who is behind this?" Kathryn added, hoping this would not delay her getting home—and that it would not irritate Linnette too much. Kathryn owed her for the advice she had given and would do what was needed to help the situation.

"Yes, Elizabeth, why don't you show me this print that has you so upset? I know we have had our differences recently, but surely we do not need to air them here." Linnette glanced at Annabelle and her sister.

"I am sure you would say that. I still cannot believe you think you can keep this a secret." Elizabeth waved the paper in the air one more time and then thrust it on the table in front of Linnette. "Here."

Linnette glanced at it and lost all color in the blink of an eye. She grabbed at the print, pulling it towards her, her gaze glued to it. "It's not true." Her voice was little more than a whisper.

"Of course, you would say that." Elizabeth reached for the print again, but Linnette held it firmly.

"You can't show it to them. It's not true. I don't know why somebody would do this, but it's not true."

"I know you slept with him in the past—why not now? I cannot believe even you would betray her like this."

"Why don't you show us this print?" It was Lucille, Annabelle's sister, who spoke up. She stood and walked to Elizabeth. "The other print was just put up this morning. I can't believe there's another one so soon. There shouldn't be one for several more days."

"Here, take a look. There's no hiding it now. Even if this is the first copy, it will be all about London within days," Elizabeth said, grabbing the print from Linnette and thrusting it at Lucille.

Taking the print, it was Lucille's turn to pale. "This can't be right. Who ever would have done this? It can't be the same artist. Look, it's not nearly as finely drawn. How can this have happened?" She looked up at Linnette with troubled eyes. "And who is the man? I know I've seen him before, but I can't remember where. This is just awful."

Annabelle came and stared over her sister's shoulder. "Oh—oh." Her gaze went to Kathryn instead of Linnette. "Why don't we just rip it apart? I don't think we need to waste time on this now, not now." Her tone was almost beseeching.

Elizabeth stood firm. "No, I think we need to deal with it now. Putting it off will not help any of us."

"But, it's not true. It's just not true." Linnette repeated it like a refrain. Kathryn was almost afraid she was going to faint.

She rose and went to stand beside her friend. "Do you want me to take you home? You are looking quite ill." Curiosity was eating at her to see the print, but friendship came first. Nasty things had been said about Linnette in the past—although only quietly. Her friend was too beautiful and too rich not to inspire jealousy.

Linnette looked at her with sudden hope. "Yes, why don't we—"

"Oh dear. Oh dear." Annie's voice added to the cacophony. Was everybody determined to repeat their words?

"Don't you think she needs to know?" Elizabeth spoke over the others, although whom her question was directed at was unclear.

Linnette stood, her back straight, her face made of stone. "Show it to her," she spat the words as she turned to face Elizabeth. "You are correct that it cannot be hidden—regardless that it is a lie. I wouldn't be surprised to learn that you are behind it. You certainly seem to take joy it. Do you know how it will hurt her—and needlessly?"

Elizabeth turned, her eyes on Kathryn, and for the first time she looked uncertain. "No, I take no joy it. And I certainly had nothing to do with it beyond seeing it in the window. You should have told her years ago."

"There is nothing to tell," Linnette answered.

"But, there was. Do you think she will feel that it is nothing?" Elizabeth would not let it go.

"What is going on? Show me the darn thing so that I can understand. I feel like I am playing blindman's bluff all by myself." Kathryn stepped away from Linnette, and toward Lucille who still held the print, Annie and Annabelle looking over her shoulder.

Lucille moved to hand her the piece of paper, but Annie reached out and took it. "I'll show it to her. One of us has to."

The four other women stood straight and still as Annie walked toward Kathryn, the print clutched in her hand, her fingers wrinkling the paper. Linnette looked like she wanted to cry.

Annie paused just in front of her—hesitated—then held it out. She also looked like she wanted to cry—or run away as far and fast as she could. "Here." Her voice held a note of bravery as she handed the print to Kathryn.

And then Kathryn's world ended.

The first glance was awful, but not for her. It showed a woman, clearly Linnette, with a hugely pregnant belly. Kathryn glanced at her friend, her eyes filled with sympathy. Linnette with child? But who was the father? Would he marry her?

And then Kathryn's eyes fell back on the paper clutched in her hand, looked behind Linnette and her belly, to the man who stood behind her, his hands on her shoulders, his dark eyes full of lust, his tall frame diminished in the drawing—but still distinctly recognizable. For a moment she could only stare, her heart full of disbelief.

She lifted her head and stared at the stony line of her friends.

She met Lucille's glance.

"The man," Kathryn said, as all her hopes died, "is the Duke of Harrington. He is my husband."

Chapter Nine

"Then that's what it means—the print's caption, *She may be a real duchess, but who's her real duke?*" Lucille whispered the words as if to herself.

Robert and Linnette? Kathryn ignored all else and took a step nearer to her friend. "Is it true? Did you sleep with—have intimate relations with my husband?" An even more horrible thought took her. Robert and Linnette had known each other since childhood. "Is he the man you were talking about, your first love who you've found again? How could you do this? How could you do this to me?"

"It's not true. You heard me before. It is not true." Linnette held her shoulders back, her eyes met Kathryn's but there was a quiver to her lips that could not be mistaken.

"Why don't you tell her all of it?" Elizabeth asked, coldly. "She needs to know if she is going to get through the next days. Tell her about your affair with Harrington."

"So you are having an affair with my husband? I cannot believe what I confided in you. How you must have laughed." Kathryn's belly burned with bile.

"No—well, yes. But, not the way this makes it look. That

she," Linnette turned and glared at Elizabeth, "makes it sound. I did have an affair with Robert, with Harrington, but it was years ago. It was before you even met him, much less married him. He is a friend and business acquaintance now, nothing more."

"You slept with my husband—how could you?" Kathryn wanted to scream. "And you never told me. Why didn't you tell me? You introduced me to the man—and you never told me! How can you call yourself my friend and keep a secret like that?"

"How was I supposed to tell you? You leave the room whenever sex is even joked about. There was never a time that was right to tell you."

"I need to get out of here. I feel ill." Kathryn turned and raced toward the door. "I can't believe you kept this from me. I trusted you. I told you everything—more than everything. No wonder you knew what Robert liked—still likes, if this is accurate." She turned, crumpled the print into a ball, and threw it at Linnette.

Annie rushed after her, and Kathryn forced herself to stop and be calm. "Please let me go. I will be all right. I just need some time alone. How could Linnette have an affair with Robert?"

"It was years ago, everybody knows that. I would have told you if there was anything recent," Annie pleaded.

"Everybody knows. Everybody knows my dear friend and my husband were—are lovers and nobody told me, not even you, Annie?"

"It's *were*. I am sure it's *were*." Annie did not sound completely confidant. "Linnette would never do that to you. I would never have let her do that to you."

Kathryn pulled in the deepest breath that she could. "I

really need to leave now. At this moment I am not sure that I can forgive any of you—except perhaps Annabelle and Lucille. They seem innocent by lack of opportunity, if nothing else. The rest of you can go to—." She could not make herself say it even though all her body sang with fury and betrayal.

"You don't mean that." Annie sounded like she might cry.

It only made Kathryn angrier. She was the victim. She didn't want to be made to feel guilty, to feel defensive. She refused to feel any fault. "I am walking home. Please advise my coachman for me."

And then she was free. She was out the door, in the beautiful spring air—alone as she had not been alone in years. No maid. No groom. No husband. No friend.

Only herself.

She strode down the street, her pace fast and furious. Her mind spun with what she had just learned—that apparently everybody else had known for years.

Was there still an affair going on? Was that why Robert had not been coming to her bed?

Was he Linnette's true love? Was Linnette his?

The thought was distasteful but she forced herself to examine it with care.

She walked faster.

Was Linnette with child? With Robert's child?

It felt like a body blow, like a canon shell ripping through her. If it was true, she might not survive.

She was almost running now, letting her body act out the fury that filled her mind.

Oh God, she didn't think it was true. She couldn't believe it was true. They would have told her.

Somebody would have told her.

She stopped, gasping for breath—almost falling to her knees.

What now? How did she face the man she had married, the man she loved, after this?

What was left for them to say?

Seduction was certainly out now. He'd had Linnette. He'd know what a fraud Kathryn was, know she knew nothing about passion and desire.

Only—and the thought grew and filled her—she was only a fraud if she let herself be.

She was going home, going home strong—strong and angry—and then she was going to get exactly what she wanted.

He was later than he'd meant to be. Robert glanced at the clock set high on the mantel. He'd managed to find the new Duke of Doveshire and had begun an informative discussion of canals and railroads. He thought he'd made progress, but the new duke with his piercing glance was not an easy character to predict. His time among the savages in Canada had clearly left a mark.

Linnette would have her hands full if she wanted to be anything beyond a retiring dowager duchess.

And then, when he'd finished with Doveshire, several men had tried to stop him as he'd hurried home. He should probably have showed more grace in his refusals of even a moment's conversation, but he'd wanted to be home.

But enough of such thoughts, all he wanted now was his wife.

He'd worked hard all day not to think of her—largely unsuccessfully—and now it was time.

He caught himself humming as he climbed the stairs. He did hope she was still awake, although if she wasn't, he might have to wake her to pour him some port.

He smiled to himself, wondering at what point he'd reveal to her that he really didn't care for the beverage. He was a brandy man—or the occasional glass of whiskey, if someone brought a bottle back from the north.

Her door was open a crack, faint light peering through. He took that as a good sign. She never slept with the candles still lit—she didn't do anything before the candles were damped.

But that was about to change. She'd mentioned seduction and he meant to hold her to it. Seduction meant candlelight, or sunlight, or bright moonlight—well, there were games that didn't require light, but he didn't think his wife was quite there yet.

His hum turned to a whistle.

He tapped on the door and then swung it open without waiting for a reply. Should he have shaved? The thought came to him belatedly.

And then all thought stopped.

His wife sat before him, but his wife as he had never seen her before.

She'd set her chair before the fire, the light warming her features and sending dancing patterns over her dress—and what a dress. It shone crimson in the dim light of the room, rich velvet just begging to be petted. It was lower than he'd ever seen her wear, her breasts rising pale and creamy above the edging of black braid. More braid formed an intricate pattern across her chest and lower belly, ending in a deep vee just above ... His eyes followed the swirls of braid, breasts, belly, lower.

He swallowed, forcing his glance back to her face.

He couldn't see her full expression, her face lay in shadow—turned away from the fire, but he could see the gleam in her eye as she examined him, every bit as closely as he had her.

He swallowed again, breathless.

What did one say to a goddess? To a warrior goddess?

Now, why did he think that?

She was the goddess of love. She was Venus in the flesh.

"You lit a fire?" he asked. "I would have thought the night warm enough." That was inane, but at least it proved his mouth still worked and he did need it to work tonight.

"Yes, it is warm, but I felt a need to be toasty. I did not want to risk a chill, not tonight."

He had to reply—warm, toasty—there must be something he could say, something provocative. "It certainly is toasty. It feels good."

Kathryn smiled, a very slow smile that seemed to measure him from boot to crown. "I am glad you approve. The port is here." She gestured to the table next to the fire. "Would you like me to pour?"

He nodded. That was safe. One could not sound foolish with a nod.

Leaning over, Kathryn picked up the decanter and lifted it to a glass. His gaze was drawn to her low neckline, the shadow between her breasts and the hint of pink at the tip of one of the creamy swells. How did she turn to the side and yet reveal more of her bosom? There were some tricks women knew he would never understand. Not that he objected.

Kathryn turned to look at him, catching him staring at her breasts. She let her own gaze follow his, then looked up again, smiling her acknowledgment. She straightened then, holding the glass of port out before her. "Would you like a sip?"

Again he could only nod, his mouth dry with anticipation—and not for the port.

He stepped forward, his eyes focused on her.

Still smiling, Kathryn dipped a finger into the glass of port and than sucked it into her mouth, the gesture unmistakable in its promise. It stopped him in his tracks.

He pulled a deep breath into his chest, trying to gain control. What had happened to his quiet, elegant wife?

"Is there a problem? Don't you want a sip? Perhaps you think the glass is dirty. It's a pity. I only have the one. Hmmm, how else could you taste it?" She dipped her finger into the glass again. Reached towards him as if to offer him a taste, but then pulled back. She dipped the finger again. This time instead of reaching toward him, she trailed the finger across her chest, a line of deep red spirits marking her smooth flesh.

Did she mean . . . ?

She did. There was no mistaking that look.

He was not a fool, he started forward. He needed no second invitation.

And drew up short as cold, burning liquid covered his face.

For a moment, he could only blink, staring at his wife, his eyes burning.

She had tossed the port in his face. She had tossed the port in his face.

His mind repeated the fact, trying to make sense of what had just happened.

"You vile bastard. You toad. You . . . Oh, darn it all. Why don't I have a proper vocabulary for these moments? You are the lowest of the low. How could you do that and not tell me? How could you sleep with my best friend and then expect to come to my bed?" Kathryn began to stalk about the room.

He followed her movements with care. She looked in a mood to use his head for target practice.

"I don't know what you are talking about. I haven't slept with any of your friends. I haven't slept with anybody but you since our marriage. Surely you know that." He tried to calm her with reason.

She turned and glared, fire shooting from her eyes. He would be burned to a crisp if thoughts had such power.

"What has brought on this show of temper?" He tried again to be calm, to understand.

"Temper? You think this is temper? I'll tell you what brought this on—learning that my husband and my best friend had an affair, learning that she is with child and it may very well be yours. You don't bother to come to my bed to give me the child I long for, but evidently you see nothing wrong with casting your seed in other directions."

Pregnant? He'd made someone pregnant? The words were so shocking that it took him a moment to realize just how preposterous they were. He hadn't had sex with anyone but Kathryn since their marriage. He certainly could not now be accused of fatherhood—unless . . . "You are not saying that there is already a child, but that one is on the way?"

She strode over to a table and picked up a small bud vase. He could see it contained the blossom he had sent this morning, the single perfect sprout of lily of the valley. Did he need to duck?

"A child on the way—as if that matters." She stopped and stared. "Are you saying you have other children?"

"No! Well, I don't know. I cannot deny that it is possible that before we were married that I . . . I was discreet and careful, but things can happen. If, however, you are talking about somebody who is expecting now—then it is impossible. The only woman who could possibly be with child is you and even then you would be months along."

Her face turned away, as if he had struck her. "I am not with child, as you well know. No, it is Linnette who is going to have a baby."

Linnette? That didn't seem possible. She was too smart to be caught in such a trap and— "Did she say I was the father of her child?"

"No, she denies it also—but she does admit you were lovers."

He almost denied it. He wanted to deny it. He held to honesty. "When?"

"Years ago, before we even met."

He still wanted to deny it. Kathryn's face made it clear that there was no acceptable answer. "Yes, after her husband died—and only briefly. It was more comfort than anything. Doveshire had been a great friend of mine, also."

Did some of the anger leave her eyes? Did she look more accepting?

"And you think that makes it acceptable?" Her voice did not sound forgiving as she passed the vase from hand to hand.

"No," he spoke with care. "It only makes it fact. I did not

know you then, doubt I had even seen you. I have never denied that I was—was with other women before our marriage."

"But you never told me you were."

"What gentleman would? Such things are secret. You know that."

"But, Linnette? How could you not tell me about Linnette? Do you know I asked her advice on how to make you want me, how to seduce you? She could not understand why it was necessary, evidently she considers you quite a lover. I didn't understand her at the time, but now that I do, how am I supposed to feel?"

"Angry. Betrayed." He could not deny her the right to her feelings.

"Yes." It was clear that he had used her words, leaving her with none—but only for a moment. "Why did you not tell me?"

"When should I have told you? When we first met? First danced? When I asked to court you? When I asked for your hand? At the wedding? On our wedding night? Tell me when, because I do not know." He could understand her feelings, but could not find his fault. He was sorry to have hurt her once again, but he could see no answer. "If I had known how my life would proceed, I would not have slept with her, no matter how great the desire, but I did not know. Knowing only what I did then, I would do the same thing again."

"You would?" Her voice was still tinged with anger, but she sounded unsure.

He raked his fingers through his hair, not caring of the curling mess he would create. "I want to say no, but yes."

"And it is not your child? You were not her first lover?"

He was not quite sure where the second question had come

from but he answered with seriousness. "No, it is not my child, and I can assure you that at least Doveshire was before me. I do not think she was widely experienced, but I was most definitely not her first."

Kathryn moved the vase from hand to hand again, but this time with more uncertainty, as if she did not know what to do with it now.

They stood staring at each other; what was to come next unclear. Her fury was gone, but she looked a long way from forgiveness, a long way from seduction.

As if sensing the need for distraction, a quiet tap sounded on the door. "Excuse me, your grace."

They both answered "yes" at the same moment. The first slight, but genuine smile of the evening lit upon Kathryn's lips.

Kathryn watched as the door cracked open, and Mr. Johns poked his head through, his eyes on the floor as if afraid of what he might see.

He nodded in Robert's general direction. "I am very sorry to bother you at this hour, your grace." Mr. Johns's face was turning redder by the moment. "But there's been a great problem downstairs with, ummm, with the delivery you sent for earlier."

"Delivery?" Robert's tone was as flat as she felt.

Her anger was fast dissipating and she wasn't sure what would take its place. Mostly she felt empty, void inside. Her hopes and dreams of this morning seemed so far away. How could she take Linnette's advice now? Did she even wish to seduce her husband?

She turned and looked him over. His beard was starting to show, a dark shadow upon his cheek. How would that feel against her skin? He'd always come to bed fresh shaven. Had he been so eager?

The beginnings of an ache began deep in her belly—could anger turn to the beginnings of desire so fast?

"Umm. Yes, the delivery from Lord Smokesly."

"Oh, blast." Robert shot her a look asking forgiveness for his curse—as if that mattered now. "I had forgotten. I don't understand how there can be a problem. Can't you just keep it in the kitchen until morning and then I will deal with it. Now hardly seems to be the time to trouble me with it."

"Well, the kitchen is the problem." Mr. Johns still stared at his feet. "I am afraid your delivery has devoured most of the larder. Two joints of beef, a pork roast, all the bacon and kippers, everything the fish man delivered and three dozen eggs. Cook is threatening to quit and the maids are either crying or laughing—and that thing is running circles about us all. I am afraid that by morning it will eat us also."

"A puppy? A small, sweet little puppy?" Robert looked perplexed, his brows drawing together to form a furrow.

"That is no puppy. I believe it may be a small horse." Mr. Johns spoke with far more vigor than usual.

"Lord Smokesly assured me that his wife's dog had delivered the most wonderful puppies. It was work to persuade him to send me one."

Mr. Johns only pressed his lips tight.

Sighing to herself Kathryn stepped forward. "And, my husband, did it occur to you to inquire as to what variety of dogs they might be?"

"Well, no. It's a puppy from his wife's dog. How different can a puppy be?"

"You do remember that Lord Smokesly married that Russian princess, don't you?"

"Yes." Understanding began to show on Robert's face.

"I do believe she raises wolfhounds. Some fierce breed from the far north."

"Dammit all." Robert turned and stared into the fire.

"Mr. Johns, perhaps the dog could be tied in the back garden for the night. I relieve you of any responsibility for what may happen to the plantings. And perhaps one of the stable boys would care to sleep out with the beas—, dog, in case it gets lonely. That is not a command, mind you. I just thought one of the lads might find it an adventure."

"Yes, your grace." Mr. Johns hurried out, clearly glad to have a solution handed to him.

"And Mr. Johns," she called after.

He halted. "Yes, your grace?"

"Tell Cook we will be fine with toasted bread in the morning—assuming that it has not been devoured also."

Mr. Johns nodded and left. The door shut with a click.

Kathryn turned to her husband. "And what, pray tell, were you doing acquiring a wolfhound? If it's the size of a pony now, I cannot even imagine how big it will be—I should have asked Mr. Johns about its feet. They do say that is how you know how large something will grow."

"I bought it for you." Robert sounded as if he were choking on the words.

"What?"

"I thought you would like a puppy. You mentioned something this morning. I got it for you."

"You got me a wolfhound?" What did a woman say to that?

"I didn't know it would be a wolfhound. I was thinking something small and sweet. I should have paid more attention, but I was distracted."

"By railroads and canals?"

"By you. I kept thinking about tonight. It made it difficult to accomplish anything today."

Her heart warmed at that—among other spots. "And so you got me a puppy—a wolfhound. I have always wanted a dog."

"I am glad. I knew it would not solve everything between us, but I want you to have everything your heart desires."

"Damn you, Robert."

He looked shocked at her words. "What have I done now?"

"I wanted to be angry for longer. I am not ready to forgive you yet. I had worked up such a good fury and now . . ."

"And now?"

"And now I don't know what to do. I can't be angry with a man who's gotten me a puppy—even if it did eat my breakfast. But I don't know what else to do." She paused. "And I still don't feel able to take Linnette's advice. It just seems wrong now."

He took a step toward her. "Forgive my bluntness. I truly do not wish to say the wrong thing, but are you not ready for seduction—which I could understand after everything—or do you not want to take Linnette's advice?"

Turning away she stared down at her hands. She didn't want to let this night pass—not if hope could be found again.

And, in truth, the fighting and the fury had left her full of energy, energy that needed someplace to go. "I am not sure. I do know I don't want to use what Linnette told me, not tonight, and without that I am lost."

He took another step, reached out and held her shoulders, the bare skin of his hands warming her own skin above the low cut of her dress. She closed her eyes and breathed in, smelling the scent of leather, smoke, and brandy that was her husband—and below all that the smell of skin, his skin.

"Open your eyes and look at me," he commanded gently. "If you are unsure how to proceed, then perhaps it is my turn to seduce my wife."

Robert watched Kathryn's eyes dilate and her breath slow. He could almost see her thoughts. She was tempted, very tempted, but something held her back. He rubbed his thumbs across the bare skin of her shoulders, her skin like velvet beneath his touch.

Her breath held for a moment, and then her chest filled, drawing his gaze to the deep cleft between her breasts. He longed to bury his face there, to pull her scent in, to . . .

She was not ready for that, she was pliant to his touch, but still unsure, her eyes stared up at him, questioning.

"We can go as slowly as you want. Anything you tell me I will listen to," he said, stroking with his thumbs again.

"I—I am not sure. I don't know . . ."

"Then why don't we take it even slower? If you sit again, this time I will pour you a glass of port, warm it between my hands, and then serve you gentle sips. A single drink cannot be bad, can it?"

"As long as it truly is only one. I do not want a repeat of last night. It took all morning for me to feel myself. I did not drink any wine at dinner." She pulled slightly away and moved back toward her chair. He kept one hand on her shoulder and followed.

Sitting, she spread her skirts about her.

"Are you trying to protect yourself from me?" he asked.

"What?"

"You've spread your skirts so far there's no room for me—unless I stand behind."

"Oh, I can—"

"No, it is fine. I will be comfortable here. I can give you sips over your shoulder." Perhaps it was best if she could not see his face, could not see the desire and longing, the fight for control.

He bent over her, reaching for the decanter of port, trying to keep his eyes from her breasts. He needed control, needed it now. Pouring a half glass, he started to bring it to her lips, and then paused. Memories of her earlier actions came to him.

He dipped a finger in the rich, dark liquid, the sweet, fruity smell rising to his nostrils. "We should be very careful that you don't drink too much. A second night of imbibing can be far worse than the first. We'll start with just a taste."

He brought his hand around her head, rubbing his finger against the fullness of her lips, but did not seek entry. "Taste," he whispered.

He heard her intake of breath, imagined her tongue reaching out to lick her lips.

He repeated the gesture, but hesitated so that her tongue caressed his finger.

The third time, he ran the wine against the crease of her mouth, waiting for her lips to part.

He pulled back as they did, barely brushing the moist skin of her inner lip.

Her shoulders quivered against him, he could feel her want beginning to grow.

He dipped again, smeared her lips again—not allowing her mouth to capture his finger.

And again.

"May I have a taste?" he asked.

"Of course." Her voice was not quite steady.

He bent forward, pulling slightly back on her shoulders with one hand. She moved with ease, her body lax beneath his touch. He brushed the rich port across her mouth, leaned forward—and tasted it straight from her lips.

He felt the first moment of her shock, the sudden intake of her breath, and then she relaxed, her mouth soft and pliant beneath his. He held his lips still for a moment, just pressing mouths together, and then slowly slipped his tongue out, licking the last drops of port from her mouth.

Waiting for the beginning of her response, the slight pucker, the parting of lips, he pulled back, stopping inches away, staring down at her closed eyes until they slowly drifted open, her pupils unfocused.

Her gaze sharpened suddenly, seeing him. He smiled and leaned back, pausing to lay a soft kiss on her bare shoulder.

He took a moment to pull several deep breaths into his

lungs. Her innocent response would be his undoing. He shifted slightly, trying to ease the building pressure.

Her head started to turn back, toward him, her eyes almost level with . . . He quickly dipped his finger in the port again and brought it forward, rubbing, stroking, moving over her lips.

"Open your mouth," he whispered in her delicate ear, his eyes drawn to its perfect arch and curve.

He dipped his finger again and this time slipped it between her parted lips, stroking the soft inner curve of her cheek. Her lips tightened about him, drawing his finger deeper. He withdrew slightly, then slipped forward again, the intimacy of the movement causing his body to clench as his mind filled with images.

God, he wanted her, wanted her now. It took every inch of will he had not to release the beast, not to pull her into his arms, to carry her to the bed, to push up her skirts, to—

Control. Control. Keep it slow.

She mewed softly, a low sound of need, her face once again turning, seeking.

Resting his hands lightly on her shoulders, he began to knead, to massage, to ease every remaining kink and bit of tightness from her. Obediently her head fell back, the crown resting against his belly just above the waist of his pants.

He swallowed, but kept his fingers moving, stroking, tantalizing.

"I am getting warm." Her voice was gentle and breathy.

"Only just getting?"

"I think . . . She hesitated. "I think that perhaps I should loosen my dress. It is very snug. I would feel much cooler if it were not so tight. I feel it pressing against me, the braid so binding against my . . . my breasts."

He could feel what the words cost her, how difficult they were to say. "Are you sure?" he asked.

"Yes." It came out as a purr.

He kept kneading for another moment and then let his hands drift down her shoulders and back to the top of her ties. He worked quickly at the knot and lacings, watching as the crimson velvet slowly slipped lower, revealing the top of her chemise and corset.

"That feels wonderful." Now it was a small moan that escaped her lips.

"I am glad." Laces untied, he slipped his hands back up her shoulders, stopping for a bit more massage, before slowly trailing them forward, across her collarbones. He paused at the top of her chemise, running a finger back and forth under the very edge of the lace, giving her time to protest—she did not.

He lightly ran his palms over the full curve of her breasts, covered now only by fine cloth, feeling her peaked nipples against his skin. Forcing himself not to tarry too long, he pushed the gown further down until only thin linen covered her above her corset, the dusky peaks visible through the translucent fabric. "Should I unlace your corset? You might breath easier. You seem a trifle breathless."

"Please." Her eyes were shut, the dark lashes a shadow against her pale skin, her head still resting against his stomach.

He cupped her breast again, squeezed once, firmly but not hard, then ran his hands back across her arms until he reached the remaining laces of her corset. It was the work of only a moment to unfasten them, to pull the straps of the corset down, to free her completely, corset and gown pooled about her waist.

His own breathing was difficult now. For the first time he was able to look upon her breasts and let his eyes feast. They were still partially veiled, but the glow of the fire lit them in a way that left his mouth dry.

He placed his hands back on her shoulders, forcing them to stillness, letting her grow used to her near nakedness. She rubbed her head back and forth across his belly. It was his turn to moan.

Her eyes opened and stared up at him, almost black with desire.

She caught his gaze and her own followed his down until she stared at her own breasts. Her hands rose and covered them, but then slid lower drawing the thin fabric tight. Her glance returned to his and for a moment he could see a deep womanly knowledge in them. She moved her head against him.

Again, rugged sounds were drawn from his lips.

"Do you like them?" Her question was real, the uncertainty there in her gaze.

"If you moved the crown of your head an inch lower, you would not have to ask."

And then she did. He was not sure what sensation she felt, but for him it was a brush with heaven.

"Should I stand now?" Again she sounded unsure.

"If it would please you." Please her. He must remember this was all about pleasing her, seducing her. His own needs must come second. In truth, he wanted her to stay where she was, her head pressed firmly against him, his arousal cushioned in the soft spill of her curls.

Slowly, oh so slowly, she pulled away from him, and half turning in the chair she rose to her feet, slightly unsteady.

And then she was standing, her gown falling to her feet, and he could not regret her movement. He'd always known she was beautiful, but now, now with the warmth of the fire glowing upon her, the thin linen showing as much as it hid, she was a goddess come to earth. He wanted to fall on his knees and worship, to press his face against the soft curve of her belly, to . . .

"Is this right? I don't really know what to do," Kathryn said, playing with a fold in the linen.

"Yes, it's exactly right," he replied, his voice gruff. "If it makes you happy. It's only right if it makes you happy."

Chapter Ten

If it made her happy? Kathryn considered the phrase. She'd never really considered whether things made her happy—and certainly not this.

And it did make her happy. Even after all the events of the day and evening, as she watched Robert she felt a bubble of joy begin to grow within her—and that was not even considering the other feelings that were slowly overtaking her.

Linnette—oh, she wasn't going to think of her now—had mentioned a tingle and there was definitely a tingle, although it was rapidly growing into a true ache—an ache that sought release.

"I do like the warmth of the fire," she answered, after a moment, looking down at her hands, suddenly shy beneath the intensity of his gaze. Who had known a man's desire could feel so powerful?

"Is that all you like?" Robert took a step forward.

What did she say to that? Her fingers pleated the fabric with more vigor. "I don't know."

He took another half-step, and then paused, considering

her words. "Let me ask differently—is there anything you don't like? Or anything else you want?"

"There is nothing I don't like, but as for the rest, I don't know what else I want. What else I should want."

Her gaze lifted as high as his chest. She watched as it rose and fell, feeling a desire to rest her hand against it, to feel the movement, to feel his warmth. Did she dare?

Her arm rose. She inched forward.

"Go ahead. Do what you wish," he said, sensing her hesitation.

Pressing her hand against him, she felt the hard planes of his chest. She wasn't sure she'd ever touched him before. Yes, their bodies had pressed together, their hands had touched, she'd held his arm, but never before had she touched him for no other reason than that she wanted to, that she needed to. The fine weave of his shirt was soft beneath her finger, his heartbeat fast, but steady. She rubbed her fingers, reveling in her freedom. It was such a small thing, but it melted something within that she had not even known was frozen.

"Can I—can I undo a button, feel your skin?" She wondered at her own bravery as she asked.

"You can open as many as you want. Do you want to remove my cravat?"

She stared up at the intricate knot. "Would you?"

It was off in a matter of seconds. His neck was beautiful. She'd never even noticed before and now she could not move her eyes away. His Adam's apple bobbed as he swallowed. She reached up and stroked it, her hand brushing the stubble of his chin.

His body stiffened beneath her touch, each muscle drawing tight.

She stopped moving. "Did I do something wrong?"

"No, if anything it is too right."

Too right? She was doing things too right. She gazed into his dark eyes and felt the truth of his words, saw the effect she was having on him. "Did you want another taste of port?"

Without waiting for his answer she turned and picked up the glass, dipping her own finger into it. She started to reach for his lips, but then brought her hand to her own mouth, following his past gesture. She wet her lips and waited.

His gaze dropped to her lips, and then back to her eyes. He held there for a moment and the breath left her body as his gaze dropped again.

His tongue darted out and dampened his own lips before he slowly leaned forward and pressed his mouth against hers, his lips firm.

His tongue darted out again, tracing the bow of her lips. "So sweet," he murmured, his mouth never leaving hers.

She felt herself soften against him, her mouth as pliant as beeswax on a July day.

When his tongue moved between her lips seeking entrance she opened, her mind filled with possibilities. He swept the inside of her mouth, her own tongue moving to meet his, to dance with his. She had never known there could be such delight in a kiss.

For a moment she let herself lose all thought, nothing existed except darting tongues and soft moist cheeks. Her lips pressed against his harder, and harder. This was all she had wanted, all she had imagined—only now she wanted more.

When his arms came around her, pressing her hips into his thighs, her belly against his hardness, she could only moan in pleasure. She rubbed herself back and forth seeking something, she did not know what, but something—something that grew and ached and demanded.

His hands cupped her behind, squeezing, rubbing, lifting.

Her feet were off the ground, her legs rising to wrap about him. She pushed closer, pressed closer, seeking more.

The kiss was enveloping now, wet and wild and devouring.

Her hands slipped through the open neck of his shirt, gliding over the silk of his shoulders, feeling the chorded muscles beneath.

Her back was against the wall now, although she was not sure when they had moved. The coolness of the plaster contrasted with the heat of his chest, of his—her mind tried to find a word that did not sound silly—none of the terms her mother had used had anything to do with what was pressed against her, rubbing her, finding some spot between her legs that caught fire, burning through her belly—demanding, always demanding more. She pushed against him further, grinding against him, trying to find that which remained just beyond her grasp.

And then she was standing, cold and alone.

She looked at him, gasping, wanting, wondering what she had done wrong, what had caused the exile from the wonder of his heat, of his arms.

He was gasping also, his breath coming in quick, jerking inhales. His brow was damp with sweat, his eyes glazed. "Give me a moment, just a moment."

Her glance dropped to the floor as again uncertainty filled her—and then she lifted her eyes. There was no winning if she did not ask. "Why did you stop? I did not want you to stop."

God, her innocent question almost sent him over the edge, an edge he was barely clinging to. It had been all he could do not to push up her chemise, to open the fall of his trousers, to take her against the wall with no thought for her near innocence, hell, with no thought at all. His body still ached for it—and his mind also. The thought of her moving beneath him, moving with an urgency and skill he had never even dreamed of from his demur wife was almost too much.

He pulled a huge breath into his lungs, concentrating on nothing but the burn, the need to release the air—and still he held it, forcing his mind and body to compliance—and then he exhaled, long and slow. "I could not take any more, bear anymore. If I had not set you away then, I would have taken you hard and fast and with no thought but my own pleasure."

"I would not have minded." Her color rose, but she continued to speak, her gaze steady. "I liked what you were doing. It made me burn here and—and here." She brushed her hand first over her breasts and then lower, across the soft dark curls he could see beneath her shift.

He closed his eyes, fought the urge to do just what her words suggested. "But you should mind—at least for now. There is a place for mindless passion—quite a wonderful place—but this is not it. This night is for gentle seduction."

"And if I do not want gentle? If I want hard and fast?"

She was trying to kill him. There was no question about

it. His heart would burst from his chest in another moment. "Then I am afraid you will have to live with what I choose to do. Tonight I want to show you all that can be. I will not risk another mistake."

"And if I insist?" She stepped toward him, her hips swaying in unmistakable invitation—and—and—no, she wouldn't—yes, she had. The chemise fell to the floor in a pool of white, leaving her bare to his gaze.

How could his greatest dream be such torture? He stared and stared, committing each inch of her to memory, uptilted, peach-tipped breasts—slim waist—slender, yet curved hips—that dark thatch of curls—slight moisture marking her firm thighs. His hands curved into fists with the effort not to reach out and touch—no, not touch, grab, and devour. He could taste her breast upon his tongue, feel the dampness between her legs upon his fingers.

No, the beast must be controlled.

And then she moved again, her legs parting as she walked—there was no hope for him.

He grabbed her shoulders, holding her back. "Do you trust me?" he asked, his voice brusque and hoarse.

She tried to push forward, her hands reaching out to stroke his chest. Her fingers circled a nipple and then moved lower . . .

"Do you trust me?" He moved beyond her grasp, glad of his long arms.

Her eyes lifted to his, her lower lip pouting. "Of course—now let me closer."

In one move he swung her into his arms, grabbing the cravat that lay over the back of the chair. He carried her to the bed and tossed her down so that she lay sprawled in the center. "Do you trust me?" He felt compelled to ask it one last time.

She lay there naked—and wanting. He could feel the need coming from her in a physical wave.

He wanted to proclaim his victory. This was his wife. His wife wanted him.

The perfect duchess banished.

She started to slide toward him, and he stepped back. "Do you trust me, Kathryn? Answer."

She stopped, and looked at him. He could see the serious thought behind her eyes. "Yes, Robert. I do trust you. I would not be here if I did not."

That was all he needed. He reached forward, grabbing her wrists as they rose toward him, pulling them high over her head, pulling her back against the pillows. He placed a quick—but not gentle—kiss upon her lips, distracting her as he quickly tied her hands to the slender wood rod that ran across the headboard of the bed.

"What?" She tried to push up, to sit. Her hands constrained the movement.

"Remember you trust me." He slid off the bed, quickly doffing shoes, and shirt and trousers—until he stood as bare as she was. Ah, that distracted her.

Her glance slid low, and stopped, her eyes widening.

"Do you know I've never . . ." Her voice was barely audible.

"Never what?" His own eyes were busy devouring her. He'd never realized how slight she was beneath her clothes—and yet so lush, plump thighs and round hips.

"I've never seen your male organ."

"My what?"

"You know exactly what I mean." And her eyes certainly let him know what she meant, her gaze never leaving him.

He felt himself swell further—which he had not thought possible. "My cock. I refer to it as a cock." He dropped his hand and stroked himself once, granting both relief and further agony. A single drop of liquid formed at the tip.

She licked her lips.

He dropped his hand, drew in another deep breath and held it. *She doesn't know what she doing, what she's implying.* He blocked the image from his mind, denied his desire to explore every inch of her soft, deep mouth.

He climbed onto the bed, pulling her legs apart and kneeling between them, her knees propped by his sides.

He stared at her face for a moment, memorizing the light sheen that marked her temples, the high color of her cheeks, the softness of her lips—no, do not think about her lips—do not think about her lips. He looked deep into her eyes, seeing the desire and the honesty.

He loved her. He had known it from the first, but as he watched her, full of desire and innocence, he felt his heart grow full. He had asked if she trusted him and he now he realized just how fully he trusted her, how much he offered her, how much he wished to give her.

He had fallen in love with her beauty, but it was not that which held him now—now it was just her, the whole her.

He leaned forward and laid a sweet kiss upon her mouth and—and said the words. "I love you."

Her eyes opened wide, staring into his own. He felt her moment of shock and then the smile that filled her face. "And

I love you too, Robert. I didn't realize how much I needed this, needed to know how you felt—and how freeing it would be." She pulled at the tie above her head. "Now free me, so that we can—"

"No."

"But—"

"I will free you but not now. There is too much I want to do to you now, too much I want to show you. I wish you could know how I feel seeing you like this, bound and helpless and all mine. I feel the beast for saying it, for feeling it, but I love knowing that you are mine, mine to do as I want with, to please as I want."

He watched her swallow, watched her grow nervous—and yet felt the tightening of her thighs about his hips, the increase of her desire. "And what I want now," he continued, "is to teach you about your breasts. You've kept them hidden by linen and by darkness and now they are mine." He placed a palm over each breast, leaning forward and allowing a fraction of his weight to fall upon them. He squeezed, and pulled, and squeezed again, watching the reactions play upon her face, the intake of breath, the further flush of cheeks.

Sliding his hands up, he pulled his fingers together until he held her nipples between them. He squeezed again, plucked slightly—tightening his fingers until just before the point of pain. Her breath caught and held.

"I never knew," she gasped when air finally filled her lungs again. "Why did nobody tell me?"

"So you like that, do you? What about this?" He leaned forward and flicked his tongue against one hard peak.

Her whole body shuddered. He caught the tip beneath his teeth and nipped.

She squealed—and not with pain, her thighs tightening about him drawing him closer.

He leaned more, drawing her whole nipple into his mouth, laving it with his tongue, tasting her, loving her. Her head swung back and forth upon the pillows, small moans escaping her mouth.

Caressing her other breast with his hand, he nipped again, her cries heaven to his ears.

"I wish I could reach the port. I'd love to dribble it upon you and lick every drop no matter where it might fall." He slid his hand lower, enjoying every quiver of her flesh. He circled her navel. "I'd love to drip it here. Do you know how sensitive you are?"

His lips moved down the curve of her breast, following the trail his hand had laid. He dipped his tongue into the indent of her stomach. The first curls of her thatch were under his fingers now, and he drew lazy circles, his tongue slowly moving to follow.

"And should I pour some here?" he asked, pushing her thighs wide, revealing all her secrets before him.

"No," she gasped, trying to sit, but held tight by her restraints.

"Yes," he replied. "Tonight I can do anything. And even without the port I want my taste." He drew a finger down her center, watching every clutch and shiver of legs and body, her eyes black with pleasure. He ran his finger up and down and then in small circles, only the lightest of touches, the gentlest of teases.

He bent forward, blew, watched the curls bend, watched her whole body rise in delight. And then he kissed. First, a sweet kiss, as he had placed upon her lips, and then he circled, tasted, devoured—tongue and lips combining to find her most sensitive of spots—he nipped slightly—and then laved in relief.

She was so sweet.

This was such heaven.

His slid a finger into her. She was sleek and wet and tight.

Her whole body twisted now, only his weight on her thighs holding her steady and open before him.

And then it happened—her whole body rose, her inner muscles clenching about his finger, again and again—and the cry, a sound he never thought to hear upon her lips, his name drenched in passion.

She fell back, the aftershocks still coursing through her.

CHAPTER ELEVEN

What had happened? Had the world ended? Kathryn knew that it had not, but she knew no other explanation for what had happened to her. She'd hoped to enjoy sex, but this, this was beyond any degree of comprehension.

Another spasm took her as Robert ran his tongue across her one more time.

Had he really done that? Had she really let him do that? Not that she'd had a choice. She had not understood why he had tied her hands and now she felt the deepest relief that he had.

She could never have let that happen if he hadn't—and she was glad—oh, so glad—that he had.

Could she look at him? The thought would have brought a new flush to her body if she had not already been so pink.

She opened her eyes, and peeked down at him.

He lifted his head—and grinned, his face full of pride.

She closed her eyes again. Now she was sure she was red—no longer pink, but red—as red as any cherry had ever been.

"Did you like that?" His breath tickled against her overly sensitive flesh.

"I am not even going to answer that." She kept her eyes closed.

"Then I'll have to do it again."

She felt his tongue dart out. "No—I mean..." She opened her eyes and looked at him. "I mean I want you to have a turn—" She swallowed as his gaze moved to her lips. "I mean I want you in me. I want to be filled by you. I want to watch your face when that happens to you. It's always been dark and I've never seen you. That does happen to you—doesn't it?"

He pushed up on his elbows. "Yes, it very definitely happens to me. I don't know if it's exactly the same, but it very definitely happens. In fact, I've been working very hard to not have it happen prematurely."

"Can that happen? I mean when you're not—it can happen like that?"

He blew out a long breath. "It can happen anytime—although not as often as when I was a boy. A man seeks more control."

"Oh—can I watch?"

He laughed. It started low and grew, the sound filling the room. "No—at least not tonight. Sometime I would quite adore having you watch, but not tonight. Tonight I like your other idea better—me in you."

He rose up on his knees, and positioned himself between her legs.

His—his cock was large and magnificent, full and long, the skin stretched tight across the tip. A single drop of moisture glistened there.

She felt the briefest moment of fear. It seemed impossible that it should fit within her. She knew it had before, but now as she watched him move forward, watched him place it against her it seemed impossible.

The tip pressed against her for a moment, the sensation unbelievable—and then he was in her, filling her. A single slow thrust and she felt her muscles draw tight again, felt it all begin again.

Could that happen twice in a night?

He leaned over her, his elbows locked tight, his eyes firmly upon her, his hips moving slowly. The strain was evident upon his face and yet he held himself steady, the chords in his neck outlined, his lips tight with effort. Again and again he moved, in, out. Each thrust drawing her again closer to the moment.

She didn't know if she could take it, her body would surely burst.

Her muscles clenched, tightened. Her head fell back. Her brain emptied of all but sensation.

Of all but sensation—and of him, of that steady gaze, that look of understanding and passion.

It was the look that did it.

Her whole body rose again, tightened as one again—and then it did burst, the world flying free about her in a kaleidoscope of color. She cried his name.

And he cried hers.

Nothing had ever sounded as sweet as the echo of "Kathryn" rebounding from the walls. His weight came down upon her.

The world cracked again.

And was then whole.

Her body fell loose upon the bed, the very thought of movement gone.

Breathing was all she could manage.

His arm came up, she felt the ties that bound her wrists loosened, felt herself drawn into his arms, cradled against his chest as if she were the most priceless object in the world.

They lay there together for awhile, silent and at peace. Kathryn breathed in the heavy musk that scented the air and wondered that it had taken them so long to find this place.

"I am sorry," Robert said after awhile, "sorry about the baby and that you needed me and I wasn't there."

"I am sorry too." She didn't know exactly what she was sorry about, but she knew the sentiment exactly.

"It hurt too much to talk afterwards. I couldn't believe the pain you went through. I hadn't ever considered that things could not work the way I wanted. I know these things happen, but I never considered that it could happen to me, that it could happen to you."

"It happened to us, to us. I didn't even realize how deeply I was hurt until later. At first, I just wanted to crawl into a hole and hide. I felt that I had let everybody down, myself, you— our son. He was real to me. I felt him move, imagined him in my arms, at my breast . . . and then he was gone and the world pretended he had never existed."

"I never doubted he existed—I only worried at what it had cost you. I could not bear to do that to you again."

"And I felt that I failed you. And that was without realizing how I had failed—that I never knew this existed." She waved her arm across the bed, ending in a strong hug.

"I never expected this of you. Perhaps I should have—no, that is wrong—I should not ever have expected this of you, but I should have realized that I could give this to you." He hugged her tighter, pressing her close as if he wished they were one.

She nuzzled her nose against his chest, enjoying the tickle of the hair. "I do want a child—do not doubt that. I want to hold your son and love him, to know that he is part of us."

She felt his chest still. "My son or my heir?"

The question caused her to pause. "Are they not the same—forgive me, I do understand the question, but I want both. I want our child, yours and mine. My arms are empty and I wish them filled. I love you. If I can never have another child, I will be fine, but I do long for him now. But, I must admit that I have been raised to believe that producing an heir is my sacred duty. I feel lacking that I have not done so."

"It does not matter." He rose up on one elbow, staring down at her, his face serious. "My cousins are not bad folk and they have a passel of children between them, of sons."

"I know, but I cannot change who I am, what I expect of myself."

He was silent for a moment, staring across the room into the darkness, then he looked down again—and smiled. His hand spread on her belly as if hoping that life was already forming. "Then perhaps," he said, his tone serious, "we should work further on the matter." His hand slipped lower.

She crossed her ankles, pressing her thighs tight, and placed a hand on his chest. "I have only one thought, I do wonder—and I know this is not the time—but, if you are not the father, and I do believe you are not, of Linnette's baby, then who is?"

"I. Do. Not. Care." He punctuated each word with a kiss.

And a moment later, neither did she.

The Maids

"Ooh, is that another one?" Abby's voice called to Jane from behind, causing Jane to step away from the shop's large window.

"Do you mean the one of the Dowager Duchess of Doveshire? I am surprised you haven't seen it before," Jane responded. "This one is mean — just like the last couple. And not nearly as well-drawn — not like that first one with all the duchesses. Do you really think the dowager duchess could have one in the oven? And to say that the father is a married man! My sister, Mary, saw her last week at Harrington House and didn't say anything about her belly. She is young enough, but I've never heard that she wants to marry again."

Jane's thoughts returned to the pleasure of the day to come. She wondered if she had enough pocket change for some fresh chestnuts. They were more fun in the winter but she had a hankering.

"But who's the gentleman? Do you think his shoulders are really that wide?"

"He's the Duke of Harrington. That's what makes this one so awful. I believe he loves his duchess — I think I even saw a different print of him making lovey eyes at her. I'd tell you some of the things my sister has whispered to me but they are too shocking. I can't believe that he'd have a child with another woman. If he is the father, I think that's just horrible."

"No," Abby said. "I saw that one days ago. Look more closely. The cartoon is almost the same, but this time it's a different man. The pose is the same, and it looks like he's wearing a ducal coronet, but it's not Harrington. This one looks like a man who's worked hard in his life."

Jane peered more closely, thoughts of chestnuts forgotten. "Oh, my! I see what you mean. No, I don't know who he is. Maybe Mary will know."

"Why would they show the dowager duchess with two different men? Do you think she's been sleeping with both?"

"I told you, I don't believe she was sleeping with Harrington — although it would be a good bit of gossip if she was. Can you imagine two men?"

"I have trouble when I even think about one. Cook always says that's what men are — trouble."

Jane thought about her handsome footman. Lady Smythe-Burke did like a footman with a well-shaped leg. "You may be right about that. And," she turned to look more closely at the print, "I would like to know who he is. You are right about the coronet — hmm, what duke aren't we thinking of? I thought I'd learned them all by sight — at least the way they look in cartoons."

Abby suddenly grew very still. She turned to Jane with wide eyes. "You don't suppose he could be . . . "

Linnette

Linnette stared down at the print that lay in the corner of her breakfast tray. She felt the gorge rising in her stomach.

It couldn't be. Nobody knew!

How could this have happened?

"I am so sorry, your grace." Her maid's quiet voice came from her bedside. "I saw it this morning when I stepped out for a breath of air. I hated to bring it to you, but..."

"No, you did the right thing." Linnette swallowed, fighting the bitter burn in the back of her throat. "Bring me paper. I must send a note to him."

Carol did as she requested and within moments the note was written, summoning him. She handed it to Carol and then turned back to the print.

She placed a finger on it, tracing the strong curve of his arm.

She didn't say his name even in her mind.

He was her secret, her treasure.

The gift she had been granted after all these years.

And now—now he might ruin her life.

As a secret he was the perfect lover, but as... The thought was too awful to complete.

Her gaze rose, seeking her maid's face.

As if reading her thoughts, Carol began to ramble, "I didn't say anything. I promise. I haven't even told my sister. I know how to keep a secret. Even when the last print came out—the one of you with Harrington—I didn't say a word to anyone."

"I trust you." Linnette looked back at the print. She lifted it from the tray. "Take this away. I couldn't eat a bite."

"But, your grace, you should . . ."

"Should do as I damn well please." The words were strong, but inside Linnette felt as if she were breaking into pieces.

She remembered back to that morning, years ago, when she'd found his note, known he was gone, known what she must do. She'd always thought that morning had been the worst of her life—the last morning of her childhood.

Was this moment worse? Probably not. She had reserves of strength and wisdom now, experience. She was no longer a girl to crumble.

She swung her legs out of the bed.

Elizabeth would pay. She must be behind this.

She was the only one who might know.

And no one else would be so spiteful. Nobody else would have reason.

The door closed with a click as Carol left with the tray.

She was alone—alone as she'd been since the moment she found his note.

Alone as she was now destined to be—forever.

She dressed quickly, choosing a dress she could manage without calling Carol back.

Moisture formed behind her lashes, but she held it back.

Her life might feel as if it were over, but she would never let anyone see she cared.

She didn't know if it was minutes or hours before she heard the clatter of hooves upon the cobblestones.

She walked to the window, stared down.

Her heart pounded with a second of absolute joy.

He was here.

He did not know.

She wrapped her arms about herself—and waited.

About the Author

Most days Lavinia Kent loves her life and knows that she has found her own happily-ever-after with her husband and three children But on those other days (you know which ones!), she is very glad for the wonderful romances, sensuous gowns, and tall, sexy men that fill her mind—and then her computer.

Lavinia lives in Washington, DC, with her family and an ever-changing menagerie of pets. She attended Wellesley College as an undergraduate and holds an MBA from Georgetown University.

What a Duke Wants is Lavinia's fourth book from Avon Romance. She also has a fun and sexy serial of e-novellas, *The Real Duchesses of London*, available from Avon Impulse.

She can be contacted at her website www.LaviniaKent.com or through Facebook and Twitter.